A COLLECTION OF SHORT STORIES

SEA STORIES
FROM THE ROCK

EDITED BY ELLEN CURTIS & ERIN VANCE

Library and Archives Canada Cataloguing in Publication information is available upon request.

ISBN-13: 978-1-77478-101-2

Copyright © 2022 Engen Books

Introduction © 2022 Ellen Curtis
The Day of Water and Woe © 2022 Christine Rains
Witch on the Water © 2022 Lisa M Daly
Hunting Among the Masts © 2022 Lisa M Daly
Stormslayer © 2022 Jennifer Shelby
Regeneration © 2022 Amanda Labonté
From the Depths © 2022 Stacey Oakley
Sea Change © 2022 Ash Greening
Say Goodbye Before You Go © 2022 Jai-Lynn Francis
Jonah's Ghosts © 2022 Brad Dunne
Waves Remember © 2022 Peter J Foote
Red Bay © 2022 Harrison Shimens
Wave Bound © 2022 Daniel Windeler
Battlin' Blue Men © 2022 Melissa Bishop
Cruising Depth © 2022 Shannon K Green
Dark the Moon © 2022 Bronwynn Erskine
Afterword © 2022 Erin Vance

NO PART OF THIS BOOK MAY BE REPRODUCED OR TRANSMITTED IN ANY FORM CR BY ANY MEANS, ELECTRONIC OR MECHANICAL, INCLUDING PHOTOCOPYING AND RECORDING, OR BY ANY INFORMATION STORAGE OR RETRIEVAL SYSTEM WITHOUT WRITTEN PERMISSION FROM THE COPYRIGHT HOLDER, EXCEPT FOR BRIEF PASSAGES QUOTED IN A REVIEW.

This book is a work of fiction. Names, characters, places and incidents are products of each author's imagination or are used fictitiously. Any resemblance to actual events or locales or persons living or dead is entirely coincidental.

Distributed by:
Engen Books
www.engenbooks.com
submissions@engenbooks.com
First mass market paperback printing: June 2022
Cover Image: © 2022 Graham Blair Designs

CONTENTS

Ellen Curtis
Introduction..007

Christine Rains
The Day of Water and Woe..009

Lisa M Daly
Witch on the Water..018
Hunting Among the Masts..042

Jennifer Shelby
Stormslayer...065

Amanda Labonté
Regeneration...083

Stacey Oakley
From the Depths..088

Ash Greening
Sea Change..105

Jai-Lynn Francis
Say Goodbye Before You Go..109

Brad Dunne
Jonah's Ghosts..131

Peter J Foote
Waves Remember..156

Harrison Shimens
Red Bay 173

Daniel Windeler
Wave Bound 189

Melissa Bishop
Battlin' Blue Men 208

Shannon K Green
Cruising Depth 224

Bronwynn Erskine
Dark the Moon 239

Erin Vance
Afterword 247

Graham Blair Designs
On the Cover 249

Introduction
Ellen Curtis

Ask any Newfoundlander or Labradorian, and they can tell you a story about the sea. Lives lived on the edge of the ocean are touched forever by the salt spray, the call of gulls overhead, and the crash of waves against the rocks. The sea shapes all of us, like broken glass churned in the waves until it's been polished smooth.

For each morning light that sparkles on the waves, each day the seas swell with storm, each night the moon and stars are reflected on that salt black mirror, there are stories in this collection. The authors who have crafted these stories have dredged the depths of their minds for the strange and unusual, have been buoyed by waves of inspiration, and have poured their hopes and fears onto the page. Herein are stories set against coastlines both familiar and strange, by authors long celebrated and newly emerging.

We invite you to dive in.

Ellen Curtis
Editor

Christine Rains

Christine Rains is an award-winning novelist and short story author from Southern Ontario.

Previous writing credits include the *Of Blood and Sorrow* duology, *Curse of the Hunted*, *Shudder of Specters*, and contributions to *The 13th Floor Floor Complete Collection*.

She holds four separate degrees.

The Day of Water and Woe

For years I had seen my mother do it. Every midweek morning, the Day of Water and Woe, she would go to the field to the east of our cottage and gather an armful of wildflowers. She'd then make the slippery trek down to the edge of the sea. She would stand for a while, silent with prayers, and then throw the flowers into the water.

She never asked for me or any of my siblings to help her. In fact, the few times that I offered, she always stated it was her duty and hers alone to make the offering to the sea gods. My father was a sailor, and she would have him return home to us safely.

The year of my tenth birthday, my father did not come home the day he promised. It was not so unusual for him to be a day early or a day late. One could never predict the nature of the moody sea nor the finicky sky. Yet after three days, my mother began to wring her hands too frequently. At midweek, she was up at first light and gathered an overflowing armful of wildflowers to offer to the gods. She stood down there for most of the morning, and I had to make breakfast for my younger siblings. I remember I burned the biscuits, and we didn't have enough jelly to cover up that ashy taste.

My father did not come home the next week nor the week after that. It was not unusual for sailors to disappear out in the vast oceans. We heard talk of a great squall to the south where we knew my father's ship would be passing through. He had named it Allegra after me.

After a month, our family began preparations to mourn him. It had been an emotionally hard month and, without him bringing home any pay, we were nearly out of food. One final midweek morning as I was curled up in bed with my sister, I heard the cottage door open and my mother go out to make her offering. This time, she did not pick any flowers, but gave herself instead.

Later that afternoon, my father returned home. The storm had thrown his ship off course, and he had lost his maps. Yet he managed to find a port from which he brought back some exotic fruits and spiced meats for us. He collapsed into a weeping heap upon hearing what his wife had done. Our aunt came to take care of us every time he went away after that.

When I turned sixteen, I found myself married to a sailor just like my father. He was tall and handsome, even with his hooked nose. I would kiss along the length of it as I whispered my love for him. Seth would then smile down at me, telling me he would sail the blue seas of my eyes if he could, and then we would never be apart.

The first time he went off on a ship after we were married, I left our tiny home and walked to that same field where my mother gathered wildflowers. I filled my arms and slipped a few times as I carried them down to the water's edge. My rear was bruised by the time I got there, but I made it without losing a single plant. I pictured my husband in my head, murmuring his name with love, and wished for him to be safely returned to me.

I didn't know exactly what my mother said when she had stood upon the shore, but I could not think it would be any different than that. I tossed all the brightly coloured flowers into the water as far as I could. A bunch would wash back up onto the sand, but there were those others that floated off to greater distances.

When Seth returned to me from his voyage, we was blessed with our first child. I did not tell him of the offering I made to the sea gods. He was not an overly pious man and only went to the temple if his captain wished the crew to pray for a safe journey. I'm sure I heard a few of his friends joking with him that Seth sometimes fell asleep during those prayer sessions. His snores were his pleas to the gods!

I did not consider myself overly pious, either. Yet I did go to the temple more often, entreating this goddess or that one for something. It seemed to me that women were generally more devout than men. Men you'd see on holidays or before major events like a sea voyage. Women would come for things as simple as praying for their baby to sleep soundly through the night.

To me, the great blue expanse of water was a far more beautiful temple to the gods than one made of stone could be. It is where I sent out my most heartfelt hopes and desires. Some midweek mornings, I would stand there for nearly an hour, just staring out over the shimmering waters.

As the months and years went by, I began to fancy

that I saw more in those waters than just gulls, fish, and seaweed. One morning, with my first-born, Devlin, in his basket behind me, I thought I saw a head pop out of the sea. It was most assuredly female, and her long locks floated around her to ride the gentle waves. I was not sure if we made eye contact, since she was too far away, but the flowers that made it that far from shore had disappeared.

I did not see anything again until I was pregnant with my second child. Devlin was waddling about in the sand, picking up as many shells as he could hold. I had thrown out my offering and let my heart sing to my beloved, who was gone on a long voyage. This time, there was no mistaking that my eyes met hers. Both of us had blue eyes, but hers were the colour of the deepest waters.

Having heard tales of mermaids, I thought perhaps she was such a creature and was attracted by the wildflowers that I threw into the water. Mermaids did like pretty and brightly coloured things, after all. Some men would have their boats painted with brilliant colours, in hopes of attracting mermaids. Yet the more I watched her floating there, the more I doubted my judgment.

The tales said that mermaids had simple minds, not so much smarter than dolphins. In her big eyes, I saw much wisdom. Without words, they told me that she knew I made offerings to the sea gods, and that my husband would be taken care of. A shiver had wiggled down my spine, and yet I felt a warmth of comfort from it.

She was something more than just a mermaid. I had never heard of a sea goddess, for it was a man's realm, but sea gods were known for their virility and promiscuity. I would not have been surprised if she were one of their daughters.

Unconsciously, my hand had touched my slightly swollen belly. The daughter of the sea smiled and disappeared back under the waves. There was no flick of a tail or shine of scales. She just became one with the water again.

I gave birth to a girl child not long after Seth returned. We named her Neera after my mother. When my father — who was still living and retired in a neighboring village with his brother — first saw my baby and heard her name, he wept. I was never sure if it was because he was happy for the honour that was bestowed upon my mother in the naming or because the loss of her still hurt him so.

The closest the daughter of the sea got to me was only a few months after Neera's birth. I left Devlin with my sister that midweek morning, and brought my daughter with me in a sling made of soft cotton. I made my offering, and the head popped up not thirty hands away from me. I admit, I did startle a little, but I did not scream or run away. I had often been told I was more brave-hearted than most women.

She smiled again, and this time I could see her teeth. They were like a shark's: many in number and deadly sharp. Her strange, ethereal beauty took the eye from that detail, though. Her flesh was pale with the faintest hint of blue, and her streaming hair was like strands from the night sky.

She made a motion to me which I did not understand at first. When she made it again, the elegant turning of her hand, I realized she wanted to see the baby. My heart beat just a little faster, but I took the sleeping child from her sling and faced her towards the sea.

Those big eyes gazed at the baby for a long time. I did not question it nor move to shift my arm when it started to grow numb from holding Neera in such a position. For me, the sea god's daughter had seen my husband home safely every time he had been away on a voyage. If she wished to stare at my child, then I would not protest.

Finally the ebony-haired creature made a wee noise, which did sound happy. She threw up her hands, splashing water about. A few drops landed on Neera, and then the daughter of the sea was gone.

I tenderly wiped at the salty water that had wet my baby and noted that a drop that had touched her bare ankle had left a mark. It was a brownish splotch and looked identical to the birthmark I had on my arm. I remember I used to call it a freckle because it was cuter that way, but my mother always told me it was a birthmark.

Had I been splashed upon by the sea god's daughter when I was a babe, as well?

I would never know the answer to that, and I only saw her on a rare occasion from far away after that morning.

Seth and I lived a good life. I provided him with three more sons. All our boys grew tall like their father, but unfortunately none had that marvelous hooked nose of his. I thought Neera had a hint of it in her features, but she was a feminine girl and she wouldn't dare grow a nose such as that!

It was not a year after Devlin had married that my husband did not return from his voyage. My hair had not even been kissed by sea salt yet, but they were telling me I was widowed by the sea gods. It was only a week past when he was due back. I could not declare Seth dead, and I refused to do so. I had the daughter of the sea watching him for me.

A ship with a sober crew returned, saying they saw Seth's ship go down. The waters were shallow this year from lack of rain, and it ran along a reef. It sank swiftly, as if the denizens at the bottom of the sea were hungry.

I still did not believe him to be dead. I was pitied, and told I was not accepting the truth of things. None of them could have ever loved as I loved Seth. And they did not know what I knew of the sea.

I waited anxiously for the Day of Water and Woe, and I was out at first light in the morning. Father Sun had barely kissed the sky good morning when I had my wildflowers picked, and I made the trek down to the shore.

I waded out to above my knees and threw my abundant offering as far as I could. My heart went out with the flowers, calling my beloved home. He had a family that needed him and a wife who loved him more than the sun loved the earth.

She appeared where the most flowers had landed in the water. Yellow and purple petals clung to her hair, making it seem as though she were dressed for a holiday. She glided towards me. Neither swam nor walked. I could not see if she had legs or a tail, even though the water was shallow and clear.

She stood as if waiting for something, hands clasped before her. Her long locks covered her nakedness, but it was her eyes I locked onto.

"Please, I want my husband to return home. I love him with every bit of my soul. I could not live if I lost him."

Her long fingers unlaced and swirled through the water in front of me. I saw there a shimmering image of Seth. He was lying, broken and bleeding, in a small boat. He was alone and unable to help himself. I knew all this just by seeing it in the water. I knew it as I knew my own name.

Then I also knew what I must do. Just as my mother had done many years ago.

"Take me in his stead. Send him home to our children, and take me to the sea."

She smiled then. Not one where she showed her dangerous teeth, but a sad and compassionate smile. It seemed what her pale face was made to do.

I was not afraid when she took my hands and gently pulled me to deeper waters. I was grateful that Seth would live and grow old, fishing off the docks as my father did. He would never forget me, I knew, and he would shed tears. Yet, he would live.

As I sank below the surface, looking upwards, I knew my beloved would find safe waters to take him home in the blue of my eyes.

Lisa M Daly

A native Newfoundlander, Lisa M Daly is an archaeologist, historian, professional ballroom dance instructor, crafter, and avid baker.

Previous non-fiction writing credits include essays *Sacrifice in Second World War Gander* and *An Empty Graveyard: The Victims of the 1946 AOA DC-4 Crash, Their Final Resting Place*, and *Dark Tourism*.

She made her fiction writing debut with "The Island Outside the War" in *Dystopia from the Rock*.

Lisa acted as the guest editor for the Summer 2019 Flights from the Rock collection.

In 2021 she released her first novella, *Navigating Stories*.

She currently works as the marketing director at Breakwater Books Ltd.

Witch on the Water

Charlotte felt a soft, cool breath on her face. She woke just a little, but did not open her eyes. The breath came again, soft and gentle between her eyes. In her still mostly asleep state, she heard a soft susurration, like the quiet run of cat paws.

"Scar," Charlotte thought as she started to drift back to full sleep. Then she realized she could still feel a weight across her hips. She reached down, and felt Scar's soft fur. With her touch, the cat started to purr. Charlotte opened her eyes, now suddenly very awake. Her hand still on the cat, she listened. She could hear Scar purring in her sleep, twitching slightly as if dreaming. She could hear the ship around her, creaking with the rise and fall of the waves. She could hear the ocean murmuring on this calm night. And she could faintly hear the overnight crew talking and calling to one another. She could not hear whatever just blew on her face.

Telling herself it had been a dream, Charlotte tried to close her eyes and return to sleep. Just as she started to drift away again, Scar jumped up, all four strong paws suddenly digging into Charlotte's abdomen, startling her and momentarily knocking the wind from her. Before Charlotte could react, the cat looked to her, the orange slash of fur almost glowing in the moonlight through the porthole, and sprang away, running out the door.

"Cats," Charlotte huffed to herself, and rolled over and went back to sleep.

Captain Charlotte Rose woke as the dawn light streamed into the room. She threw back the blankets and walked, or rather swayed as she was always a little unsteady on her feet for the first minutes of the day, to her door and closed it. At night, the door to her quarters was left ajar so Scar could come and go throughout the night. Now she closed it to maintain some privacy while she went about her toilette. With her face washed, her hair tucked under her hat, and her belt buckled, Charlotte opened the door and stepped into the corridor. Descending a ladder, she walked to the galley to get her breakfast of porridge and tea. The room was strangely empty, just herself and one steward keeping the kettle hot and making sure no one took too many tea leaves. She ate quickly, guessing it was going to be a difficult day and this might be her only meal for a while. Whenever her crew behaved out of the ordinary, it usually meant she was in for a long and crisis-filled day. Grabbing a fresh mug of tea, she went in search of her crew.

It didn't take her long to find people. She just followed the cacophony. A few dozen voices in a small space will carry across the ship. She found everyone still in the sleeping quarters, but not in their bunks. It was a small space, and she had to push herself through the crowd, lifting her tea in front of her.

"What's going on here? Why is no one on deck?" she demanded, her tone forceful and direct.

The crew around her started to stammer explanations, many talking to their feet or mumbling answers, but she couldn't make out exactly what was being said.

"Silence!" she spat and turned to one of the deck hands. "Dawson. You, and only you, tell me what is going on."

She waited while Dawson shuffled his feet, looked up, met her eyes for a fraction of a second, and went back to looking at his belt.

"Well, you see, it's, um," then he found his voice and looked up. "It's Mr. Jack, Captain. He's dead."

"Dead?" Charlotte asked, surprised. "What happened?"

Again, the room erupted into murmurs as half the crew tried to answer.

"Hush! Dawson, please tell me what happened." She softened her tone. After all, this wasn't her crew simply not doing their jobs; a death would rightfully shake them.

"We don't know, Captain," Dawson replied. "He just didn't wake up this morning."

"Let me through. Let me see," Charlotte ordered the group at large. Her crew tried to make space. "And has anyone called the medic?"

The tone of the crowd suggested they hadn't. Charlotte took a breath and wondered why she had to be the first to think of that.

"Who's next to the door? Wilson? Go get the medic," she ordered.

She made her way to Jack's bunk. The deckhand was

dead, the medic wouldn't help at all. His skin was ashen and his face contorted in a scream. His eyes bulged and his mouth was opened with his teeth bared. His hands were up and in front of his body, trying to push away whatever scared him.

"Who found him?" Charlotte demanded.

"I did, Captain," said her navigator, Collins.

"And you found him like this?" she asked.

"Yes, Captain," Collins replied. "He was due on deck and when he didn't show, I came down to get him. He was just like this, frozen. I wouldn't even touch him like that."

Charlotte stared at the man, unable to look away from the terror in his eyes.

"Let me through!" came a shout from behind Charlotte. It was authoritative and the crowd parted to let the medic through. Hazel walked through, carrying a battered bag of medical supplies. Scar followed in her wake.

"Why are all these people milling around?" she asked Charlotte.

"Yes, you're right." She had been too shocked to really react, but even with this death, there was still a ship to keep afloat. Charlotte turned to her crew who were pushing back to fill in the gap left by Hazel's arrival. With a deep breath, she bellowed, "Everyone, you're done lollygagging around. Get back to work or you'll be on bilge duty for the next fortnight!" Before she could even finish, her crew, her efficient, curious crew, started to hurry out of the room. She was a good, fair captain, but she always followed through on her threats. A captain who didn't did not get to stay captain for long.

The room was quickly empty save for herself, Hazel,

Scar, and Jack's earthly remains. Charlotte turned back to Jack, and Hazel was already bent over, examining the body. Scar walked between them and sat under Jack's bunk and started grooming.

"I was told he was found like this," she said to her medic.

"I expect he was. You can't pose a body like this," Hazel said as she poked and prodded.

"Any ideas?" Charlotte asked, taking a sip of her tea. Realizing what she was doing, she laid the cup aside.

Hazel huffed. "I've hardly gotten a look. But no, nothing I can immediately see. Poor bugger looks frightened to death. No one saw anything?"

"Of course they didn't. This many people on a ship and it's amazing how few will see anything," Charlotte replied.

Hazel straightened. "I can't tell anything from here. Get one of the hands to bring him to my office. I'll take a good look there while the sun is high and the room is bright."

"Right away." Charlotte paused, then asked, "Could he really have been scared to death? Such a thing could cause panic."

"I've heard of stranger. But, no matter what I find, we'll figure out something to tell the crew. Last thing we need are ghost stories."

Captain Rose prowled around her ship, catching sailors unaware as they stopped to gossip. She'd snap at them and they'd scatter back to their tasks. The immediate threat to her ship was gossip, and she didn't want stories to grow and spread. She'd seen gossip take down a ship as quickly as typhoid. She was a little harder on the crew than they needed, but knew it would help them focus. After weeks at sea, they could turn on each other quickly, so she found it best to focus their ire on her.

She went about her duties, confirming their location and asking her first mate about potential friendly ports and their distance. Jack wasn't an officer, but he was their best storyteller and singer, which meant they all knew him. He was fairly quiet, as far as seafolk go, but when pressed, could sing rousing songs that lifted the spirits of the crew. They'd have to give him a proper burial at sea, and make sure there was enough grog available to keep them singing and telling tales until dawn. That would be a fitting send off. And if it didn't quiet the anxieties on board, then they'd find a port and give everyone a few days shore leave.

Basic duties seen to, Charlotte went to Hazel's room.

"How's the patient?" Charlotte asked as she entered.

"Still dead," Hazel replied. "And before you ask, no, I don't know what did it, but if I had to guess, I'd say his heart."

"His heart? But then why the rictus?" Charlotte asked.

"The heart doesn't always go quietly," Hazel replied solemnly. "Sometimes the last throes are violent. I'd say that's what happened here."

"That should help ease their minds." Charlotte peered at Hazel. "Is that what you believe killed him?"

Hazel sniffed. "Looks like his heart was bigger than it should have been, but his expression still chills me. I've never seen a look like that on a corpse."

"Keep looking if you must, but we should give him a send off tonight."

"Agreed. I don't think I'll find much else, but I'll wrap him up and have him ready for sundown."

Charlotte gave Hazel a gentle pat on the shoulder.

"Thank you, my friend." As she looked back at Jack, Charlotte noticed Scar sitting under the cot turned makeshift autopsy table.

"What's with the cat?" she asked.

Hazel glanced under the bed. "No idea, but she's been there the whole time. Followed the body from the bunk."

Charlotte bent down and scratched Scar's head. "Strange thing. Go hunt mice in the stores, that's what you're here for."

With that, she stood up, turned and left the room.

The crew got loud, fast. The rare ship-board funeral usually did. There was no quiet awkwardness as people started drinking and remembering like you'd see on land. No, a ship's funeral was something different. At sundown, as each crewmember finished their work, they came to the main deck, some with instruments and all with their mugs. Charlotte had the grog prepared a little strong. This wasn't to get lemons in them, this was to get the fear out of them. Within minutes, Sammy was plucking at the strings on a harp and Leslie was beating a soft rhythm on her drum. Fred started the first story about Jack, Dawson the next. Charlotte watched from the sidelines, close enough to show her respect, but far enough into the shadows that the crew would forget about her and properly mourn. She was enjoying the stories. Jack was a storyteller after all, so they all tried to tell his stories.

Usually quiet, Jack had a rare talent to bring life to stories. Charlotte watched and wondered who would take over as storyteller. A ship had certain requirements: someone who could carry a tune, someone who could play an instrument, and a storyteller. These people kept the ship sane and helped keep order. Most didn't realize they had that role, but Charlotte knew. She was watching Alex tell of their most recent adventure and had a feeling she'd take over as storyteller.

"So we go into this run down temple. There's spiders and rats everywhere, and it looks like it's been looted a dozen times over. The pews are broken, and there was a fire in front of the alter at some point. There's not going to be anything worth our time, but we look anyway. Next thing, Jack comes out of a side room waving something shiny, and this old woman, like an honest to goodness crone, all bent and dressed in black, is following him. He waves the piece around. 'Look what I've found!' he cries while she pleads something about the relic. Jack held it high 'At least we found something in this decrepit place!' he laughed."

Alex paused as others laughed. Charlotte smiled. That gold statue had been the only thing of value in that town. She hadn't known Jack was the one who found it. Fred had delivered it to her back on the ship. Everyone had been disappointed. They had left with some fruit and dried meats, but there wasn't even enough water to refresh all their stores. They had stopped further down the coast when Dawson had spotted a freshwater stream waterfalling off a cliff. The crew had a swim and refilled the water. It made for a good distraction after a poor pillage.

Alex's story ended and another song started up. The crew would be out all night, and would eventually send the body overboard, but not until after they were all quite drunk. Charlotte quietly left the group. They couldn't really start to mourn with her there supervising. She checked on Collins at the wheel, then started for her room. On the way, she noticed Scar on top of a closed rain barrel, attention fixed on the ocean. Curious, Charlotte walked closer and followed the cat's gaze. The orange cat gave the slightest flick of her ear to acknowledge Charlotte's presence. Far off in the distance, something moved on the waves. It looked like fog. No, Charlotte looked harder. It looked like a woman dancing on the waves, the white like a gauzy dress on the wind. Charlotte shook her head and looked back at the cat, who now stared back at her. She looked to the ocean again and the figure was gone.

"Just the mist," she said quietly to reassure herself as she scratched Scar's head. "Just the mist."

The next morning, she woke to commotion. She wasn't expecting that at all. In fact, she was expecting a quiet morning while everyone sluggishly moved around trying to keep their heads intact. Scar was dashing around the room. At some point in the night, her door must have closed, trapping the cat in. Strange that the cat hadn't jumped on her to wake her.

She quickly pulled on her clothes and left the room, the cat barreling between her feet and out on to the deck. Her crew generally looked unwell, and none of them should have been awake at this hour.

"What is going on here!" she bellowed, and a few people clutched their heads and groaned. Charlotte stifled a smile. It was cruel to take pleasure in their pain.

This time Alex came forward. "It got Fred," she said, and started to cry.

"What does that even mean, 'It got Fred'?" Charlotte demanded.

Dawson spoke up: "Whatever killed Jack. It killed Fred too."

"Nonsense," she declared. "Jack's heart gave out. Where's Fred? Someone get Hazel. Nothing 'got' anyone."

Charlotte turned on her heel away from her crew and strode toward the bunks. She assumed that's where she'd find Fred. Sure enough, there he was, in his bed, arms outstretched trying to keep something away. Charlotte froze. It was just like Jack. She could see exactly why her crew was so spooked, and why they wouldn't even stay in the room this time. Fred looked terrified, just as Jack had.

Charlotte stared, and only snapped out of it when she noticed movement under Fred's bunk. Scar, sitting there staring forward.

"What is going on with you, cat?" she asked and started to bend down to touch the ship's cat when Hazel bustled into the room, carrying her medical bag.

Hazel took one look at Fred, put her bag down, and walked back to close the door. She glanced around the room again, seeing only Charlotte, Scar, and the remains of Fred, and said, "Captain, I have no idea what is happening on your ship."

Charlotte straightened up and approached her friend and confidant.

"Nor do I," she admitted. "There is something strange,

and Scar acting funny doesn't help matters. If the crew catch on, the poor cat might have to learn to swim." She sighed and looked from the cat to the body and back again. "Let's get this body out of here. I don't know that another funeral is going to help, but the crew being able to see him will only make things worse. I'll go get Collins to help move the body. Can you wrap him in a blanket while I'm gone?"

"Of course, Captain Rose," Hazel replied and started toward Fred. "Charlotte?" she turned and asked.

"Yes?"

"Conditions of the heart are not contagious. Something has to be causing this, but I'm afraid figuring that out may be well beyond my ability," Hazel confessed.

"I know. I understand," Charlotte replied solemnly. "We'll do our best."

"But I wonder if you might not be better off getting an actual physician after all this."

Charlotte approached her friend and placed a hand on her shoulder. "You grew up around medicines. You have more training at your mother's knee than most of the physicians I have met. You brew the tisanes and mix the grog that keeps this ship healthy. Plus," and here Charlotte dropped her voice, "you are my friend and confidant. This ship would be lost without you. If you want to leave, I would never stop you, but I do not doubt your ability for a moment."

Hazel looked at Charlotte. "Thank you, Captain. That means a lot." Then she turned back to Fred, her back straight and poised to face the task at hand. "Now to get him ready to be moved."

Charlotte left Hazel to her task and went to find her

first mate. He was tired from working all night while the crew had their memorial. She sent him to the bunks to help Hazel move Fred while she moved the crew to another part of the ship.

Once they gathered, Charlotte steeled herself and put on her captain voice.

"Listen up, each and every one of you," she started. "I'm sure you've all heard of what happened to Fred overnight, and are speculating that it was the same thing that happened to Jack. The truth of it is, we don't know what happened to either. It could be the same thing, it could be different things. The stress of Jack dying could have taken Fred too. We don't know. But before the stories start swirling around the ship, let me give you this option: we will make for the nearest friendly port and anyone who wants to jump ship can get out of their contract with no questions asked. We have no goods to sell, just that statue that Jack found at our last stop, which, I will remind you, was also our first stop on this trip, so you won't get a cent. But you also won't be keelhauled for abandoning the ship. I also will not put this ship into an unfriendly port which might get us all hanged for piracy, so don't even suggest such a thing. The nearest friendly port is three days out, and we'll rest there another three, so make your choice."

Charlotte paused, then added, "And I'll not have even a whisper of mutiny. For the next three days you will keep this ship running to the best of your abilities. I will not hesitate to do what needs to be done to keep this ship running in perfect order. There will be no lollygagging. That is not a luxury we have. So do your jobs. Dismissed!" she shouted the last word to let them know there would be no questions. To punctuate the moment, she turned on her heels and marched to the wheel. The crew knew better than to talk to her while at the wheel unless it was a life and death situation.

Charlotte watched the ocean and thought about the situation. They'd find a port. She'd likely lose half the crew, and would have to limp to the next port on a skeleton crew. Stories would spread fast about the ship being haunted or some such nonsense, and she wouldn't get anyone new at the first port. She'd confer with Collins to make the fastest trek to the next port, even with a smaller crew, to attempt to beat the rumours. In the meantime, stories or not, something was happening on her ship. One death wouldn't have been too bad; people die, sometimes unexpectedly. But two deaths, and in that same horrific manner... Charlotte shuddered thinking of the horror on both Jack and F'ed's faces. Fred would have to have a quieter send off, something more formal that evening. 'he'd have extra rum available, but the crew would be able to gather how they wished to talk and mourn. Another wake like they had had the evening before would only result in ghost stories and mutinous thoughts.

Charlotte was lost in thought, absently guiding the ship, when Collins returned. The two discussed what ports to call into. Finally, Charlotte had to ask him if he'd be staying on the vessel.

"Of course, Captain. I'd have nowhere else to go," he replied.

"That's not true. You're a great navigator and this ship wouldn't run without you. You could get on any ship."

"Not what I mean, Captain. I'd have nowhere else I'd want to go. I've been on this ship as long as you have. We've been through worse storms."

"Thank you, Collins. You have the wheel. I'm going to my cabin to try to figure out this disaster. I'll be back soon so you can sleep."

"Aye, Captain," he answered, and stepped forward to take the wheel.

Charlotte returned to her cabin. Scar was already in there, sitting on the edge of her desk. She took a seat and tried to pet the cat, who turned away and started digging at an open chest on the floor.

"Knock it off, cat," Charlotte said absently, and made a weak gesture as if to shoo the cat away. Scar ignored her and kept digging at the cloths and trinkets in the chest.

"I said stop, Scar. What are you digging at?" Charlotte said, frustrated at the distraction. She got up and went to the chest, while Scar kept digging. Trying to push the cat away, Charlotte gave up and instead tried to figure out what Scar was digging for. It wouldn't have been the first time the cat dropped a dead mouse somewhere inappropriate. Letting Scar guide her, Charlotte moved some silks she'd obtained on a previous trip out of the way and uncovered the statue from their last stop. Scar stopped digging, and Charlotte removed the gold piece from the chest and laid it on her desk.

Sitting again, she stared at it. Scar jumped on the desk and sat tall, looking like a statue himself.

"Ugly thing, isn't it," Charlotte said to the cat. "I don't even think it's actually gold just gold leaf or some other coating. Probably wasn't worth the stop."

She picked it up and dug a fingernail into the gold at the base, some of it easily flaked away to show the plaster underneath.

"Just as I thought," she said putting it back down.

"Worthless." She slumped over the desk and put her head in her hands. She had felt bad taking the statue from the old woman, she wasn't heartless after all, but there had been nothing to take from the village, and, as captain, she knew she had to let her crew take the statue. This trip was a disaster, and she didn't know how to fix it. Taking a deep breath, she busied herself with sea charts, trying to feel like she was doing something useful, before giving up to relieve Collins.

"We give Frederick Blanche to the sea, where he spent most of his life, having started as a stowaway on a galleon, starting a long career in doing the wrong thing. He was always gruff with his crewmates with fleeting moments of kindness. There was no one better to have at your back. He was a loyal member of the crew and we thank him for that."

Charlotte wasn't sure she had ever heard Collins say so much at one. She had asked him to speak as she wasn't sure that the crew would want to hear more from her. She'd given too many speeches, or rather ultimatums and threats, in the past two days that they didn't need to hear from her. She helped lift Fred's shrouded remains over the rail, and Collins poured some rum into the ocean after it. The crew were silent, unsure what to do next. Charlotte walked away and back to the wheel. If she went back to work, the crew would slowly follow. When they went to the mess they'd find extra drink for them, but not enough to get drunk. Collins would stick around for a while, especially if anyone wanted to talk after his eulogy.

Charlotte watched the sun set and reflect off the ocean.

It was a strangely calm sea, almost like glass. The setting sun shimmered across the water, and highlighted a point of mist. Scar appeared and jumped up on to her shoulder, looking out at the sun. No, at the mist. Charlotte squinted into the sunset, and again imagined that the mist looked like the silhouette of a woman, gossamer skirts flowing around her. Scar made a noise and Charlotte glanced at the cat. When she looked up again, the figure was closer.

"That's not how fog acts," Charlotte said softly to herself. She looked at Scar again, who was standing, his back arching just slightly, paws digging into her shoulder. Looking up again, the figure was closer. Charlotte debated ringing the ship's bell to warn everyone, but warn everyone against what? A trick of the light? Fog? Anyone worth their salt on the sea had seen strange things on the ocean. She'd never keep control of the ship if she panicked at a trick of the light. Instead, she called to a passing crewmember.

"Alex. Alex!" she called and when Alex looked up, she continued, "Fetch the medic, I want to see her immediately."

"Aye, Captain," Alex replied and hurried off.

Charlotte waited and watched the mist. Scar jumped to the railing, eyes on the water. Charlotte adjusted the course of the ship just slightly, to take them away from a direct path toward it. Easier on her eyes anyway, to not be sailing directly into the sunset. As Hazel came on deck, the mist had moved closer still, and Scar stood watching it, hackles raised.

"Captain Rose?" Hazel asked.

"See anything on the water?"

Hazel looked at Scar, and like Charlotte, followed the

cat's gaze.

"What is that?" she asked.

"So you do see it?" Charlotte responded.

"I do. It looks like someone dancing on the water. Scar doesn't like it."

"I don't either. It's been moving closer."

The sun was low to the horizon now, more of a reflection on the water than direct sunlight, and the figure started to move faster.

"Captain," Hazel said, caution in her voice. "Whatever it is, I think it's waiting for dark."

"I think so too. Advice on how to handle this?" Charlotte asked, watching the figure skate across the water.

"No. Sound the alarm maybe?"

"You think that will cause a panic?"

Hazel forced herself to look from the figure to Charlotte. "Aren't you panicking?" she asked.

Charlotte looked back at her and nodded. "Sound the alarm," she said.

Hazel stepped away from the wheel and a second later the bell tolled. Crew started to gather and all Hazel did was point. People noticed the mist, then recognized that it was moving toward them. A murmur grew to a rumble as each realized it wasn't just a trick of the mist. Voices raised as concern set in.

Collins rushed to the wheel. Without a word, Charlotte stepped away, letting him take it, and turned to her crew.

"Attention! Eyes to me!" she called, knowing they would keep darting glances at the figure. She herself fought to keep her eyes on the assembled crew. "We don't know what this is, but there is no indication that we should panic."

"It killed Jack and Fred!" someone in the gathering cried.

"We don't know that!" Charlotte said, force behind her voice. "Whatever this is, our only option is to keep the ship safe. Now, everyone, arms yourselves and get to your stations. Do not leave them unless told otherwise by an officer. Everyone keeps this ship afloat, and by the gods, we will face this thing like pirates!" With those words Charlotte raised her cutlass overhead and pumped it up and down. The crew followed suit and cried out, panic being replaced by fight and ferocity. "Now go!" she ordered, and her crew dispersed, off to protect their own little corners of the ship.

She knew her crew were fierce, and the worst this monster could have done was shown itself. However it had killed Jack and Fred involved skulking in the shadows. That caused fear. But, even as a spectral, supernatural bit of mist dancing on the waves, it was a target, a thing to be destroyed. It shouldn't have shown itself.

Charlotte gave a wry grin to her officers.

"Medic, we'll need you to be ready in case anyone needs care."

"Aye, Captain," Hazel replied. She turned on her heels and went to get her supplies, not sparing a glance to the figure on the water.

"First mate Collins, you keep this ship steering true."

"Aye, Captain," he grunted.

Only now did Charlotte look at the specter. The sun was gone, and the figure was approaching fast. A breeze floated over the ship, and on it came a voice "What's mine..." it called. The voice made Charlotte's blood run cold.

She suppressed a shiver and asked Collins, "Ever seen anything like this?"

"I've heard stories. Ghosts looking for revenge. Looking for something stolen. Always ends with a sole survivor limping back to a bar to tell the tale. I take no stock by it."

"Well, we don't have any loot, just that ugly statue."

"Miiiinnneee..." came a hiss on the wind.

Too close. Charlotte looked and the figure was off the bow. Deckhands swarmed the area, weapons raised. Charlotte heard a pop and saw the puff of smoke where someone fired on the thing, followed by more shots. The ghost didn't slow, but raised itself from the water and floated over the rail to the deck. Her pirates engaged, but their swords were useless, as effective as slicing fog. The specter thrust out an arm and passed its hand into Sammy's chest. A moment later, Sammy clutched at where the hand had been, eyes wide with fright, and fell to the deck. The fighters fought harder, while two of them pulled Sammy from the fracas and toward Hazel. Hazel placed two fingers on Sammy's neck and shook her head. The two turned back to the figure, fire in their eyes, and rejoined the fight. The woman of mist kept approaching, making its way toward the wheel.

"I come for what's MINE!" it shrieked and pointed a finger at Charlotte.

Charlotte, terrified, stamped down the panic. A thought came to her and she whispered to herself, "The statue. Jack found it, gave it to Fred, who gave it to me." Louder, she proclaimed, "It must want the statue!"

At that, Scar hissed and ran to Charlotte's cabin. Charlotte turned and ran.

"Keep my ship safe!" she called to Collins.

As she entered her cabin, Scar was leaping on the desk. Without hesitation, the cat swiped a paw at the statue, sending it flying. It hit the floor and broke. Just as Charlotte had suspected, there wasn't any gold, just white ceramic painted. But no, not just ceramic. Charlotte hurried over and picked up the pieces. Bone jutted out at the split. A finger. What had Alex said when telling the story of finding it, the old woman had called it a relic. This was a piece of someone, and that someone wanted it back.

Charlotte made certain she had every piece of the statue, and grabbed a purse from the desk. She dumped the coins on the floor, not bothering with the ones stuck in the folds of the material, and jammed the pieces of the statue into the sack. Scar hissed again and Charlotte turned to the door. The figure was in the doorframe.

Charlotte stood in awe for the briefest of moments. The woman was beautiful, her skin, hair, and dress luminous in the moonlight, seeming to carry a light of its own. Her features were not angry, as Charlotte would have guessed from its vengeful actions, but lost, almost sad. It reached toward Charlotte and Charlotte quickly looked around the room for a means of escape but the woman was between her and the door. She wondered if she could just give the ghost the remains of the relic, and thrust the bag forward. The specter reached for it, then reached past it. Charlotte could feel the cold radiate off the figure. It was going to kill her.

Just as the ghostly hand was about to touch her, Scar hissed and spit and leapt to the figure, claws out. For the barest second, it looked as if the cat had gained purchase on the woman's face, and it was enough for the spirit to step to the side, flinging her hands to her face. Charlotte took the opening, praying for Scar's well-being, and ran. As fast as she could, she ran to the stern. If it wanted the statue, it could have it. Charlotte pulled her arm back, and with everything she had, she threw the bag of bones as far into the wake of the ship as she could. She turned to see the figure racing toward her, floating across the desk with Scar giving chase. Charlotte braced herself for the cold touch of death when the figure rushed past her, a chill of breeze so cold that Charlotte shivered. The figure dropped off the stern and into the water, giving chase to the statue.

Scar leapt to the railing and stopped short, not willing to chase the ghost any further than the confines of the ship. Charlotte turned to the ocean and watched the wake for any further movement. After a few seconds, she started to absently rub Scar.

"I think we did it," she said to the cat. Scar gave a final lash to her tail and sat, continuing to keep watch.

As they approached port, Charlotte once again rallied her crew.

"I stand by my earlier statement. Any of you who want to leave are released from your contracts. I'd ask you to not spread rumours about the ship being haunted, but we all know that won't happen." There was some uncomfortable laughter. "We set sail at noon on the third day. If you are not on board, that is your choice. You may freely remove your possessions, no one on this ship will stop you. Those who come back, I thank you. Dismissed," she finalized and strode away.

Hazel appeared at her side and kept pace.

"Think they'll leave?" she asked.

"Likely. Many of them are still spooked by the whole thing. And at their hearts, they are sailors, and no one is as superstitious as a sailor," Charlotte replied.

Hazel nodded and walked away, knowing Charlotte had to focus on docking.

A few hours later, Charlotte, Hazel, and Collins braved a corner table in a tavern. They ordered food and drink, and Charlotte was just about to start in on her kidney pie when Alex approached with a young man in tow.

"Captain Rose," she said cautiously.

Charlotte looked up at the storyteller.

"This is Pascale," she continued. "He'd like a place on the ship."

Charlotte sat back in her chair, trying to mask her surprise. "Is that so," she said, slowly.

"Aye. I was telling him about how you saved us from the spirit, and he wants to join," Alex elaborated.

Charlotte leaned forward and looked at the fellow. "You got experience?" she asked.

"Aye, Captain," he stuttered a little nervously. "I was on a proper galleon as a swabbie and got left here when they caught me cheating at cards."

"How did you get caught?" she asked.

"I didn't hide me winnings and the first mate didn't like that I won his hat!" Pascale beamed and doffed his tricorner.

The trio at the table laughed at that. A little mischief always went over well on the ship.

"Alex, you'll vouch for him?" Charlotte asked.

"Aye, Captain. We knew each other on the streets a lifetime ago."

"Then we'll take you on. Come to the ship the morning before we depart and we'll find your place," Charlotte replied.

Pascale and Alex both beamed. Charlotte figured she might have to bunk them in different cabins, or else she'd be getting complaints from other crew. Seeing that they weren't leaving, Charlotte made a shooing gesture, and they turned together and left.

Charlotte was just about to cut into her pie when Leslie approached with a woman.

"Captain Rose," she asked hesitantly.

Charlotte, frustrated that her pie was getting cold, looked up at the women.

"Meredith would like to join the ship."

"Fine fine, I'm sure we'll need the hands. Bring her to the ship the morning we leave," Charlotte said, dismissing the two.

Quickly, she took a bite of her pie. She was mad at the interruptions, but confused. She swallowed and turned to Collins.

"What is happening?" she asked. "Shouldn't they be jumping ship, not bringing folks forward?"

Collins, cup halfway to his mouth, took a swallow and replied, "Captain, you saved them."

"I did no such thing," she protested. "Three of them died."

"Aye, and when the culprit appeared, you figured out why it was haunting the ship and took care of it. You kept the ship safe."

"Hmmm," she pondered and speared a piece of meat.

She took a moment to chew then asked, "So you think they're going to stick around?"

"Not just stick around, Captain. Alex is over there telling the story as we speak."

All three looked to the far corner of the room where Alex was making broad gestures, deep in the throes of storytelling.

Collins continued, "She's telling them all about how you and the cat figured out why people were dying and saved the ship. I wouldn't be surprised if you didn't have you pick of the port."

"And I bet Scar will be getting a fair bit of fresh fish and meat," Hazel added.

Charlotte pondered their words. "Guess I should hold off taking on any more hands until we go to leave. Then we'll take our pick." She grinned. "So Collins, I guess that means we don't need to rush to the next port to replace our crew. What are your thoughts for our next destination? I long for a bigger haul than an ugly, little cursed statue."

Hunting Among the Masts

"Lady Applewood, how are you enjoying your passage?"

"I would enjoy it more if I were not a captive."

"Yes, but besides that, is everything to your liking? We wouldn't want you to feel we were somehow mistreating you. That would take away from our ransom demands!" Captain Smoke gave a wicked grin, showing just enough teeth for the sun to glint off the golden one at the corner of his smirk.

"And if I did complain, what would happen then?" Midna, Lady Applewood, asked.

"Well, perhaps nothing. Then again, perhaps we would take you out of your luxury cabin, strip you down to your short clothes, and have you clean the ship. Or, maybe we could let you go. We are days from land. How well can you swim?" The captain's grin grew larger. "I think the worst we could do would be to give you to the cat."

"The cat? Why, we have been at sea for a week. I have not seen a cat on this vessel at all. For that matter, I have not seen a rat either."

"That's because the cat is the most dangerous thing on

this ship. Look up." Captain Smoke gave a nod of the head upward, to the rigging and masts. "Do you see him?"

Midna looked up, holding her hat to her head. "There is nothing up there but... Wait now, what is that moving?"

"Don't look up much do you? Most *civilized* folk don't," the captain sneered. "You'd never survive out here on a ship, never looking at the sky and the wind in the sails."

She dismissed him. "Spare me your comments on the aristocracy. Is that a cat on the mast?"

"'Tis."

"I know cats are good climbers, you will see them sometimes on the cupboards in the kitchens, but that cat is so high... How does it get down?"

"This one, it doesn't."

"Then how is threatening me with the cat really a threat? Is it just a joke?" Midna leaned back against the railing, still holding her hat, watching the cat move from one mast, through the rigging, to another.

"No joke. Though I'm not entirely sure how we'd get you up there. I mean, if we tied you in the rigging the cat might not go after ya'; no sport to that. I guess we'd have to dangle you from a mast and see what happens."

"Let's not. My cabin is perfectly fine, thank you. And my treatment has been more than adequate, though the food could be better," she said honestly.

"If you can find a better cook on a ship, I'd be happy to force them on board too!" Captain Smoke replied with a hardy laugh. "Good food on a ship, wouldn't that be a treat!"

Still laughing, the captain walked away, leaving Lady Applewood still watching the cat.

The cat was born on the ship. Her paws had never known land. She had been the runt of the litter and no one, not even her mother, thought she'd survive. She walked with her legs spread wide, looking shaky, and her fur stuck up in little tufts, like it didn't quite fit. Her mother tried to abandon her, walking away every time she tried to feed, but she managed to get enough. After all, there were only so many placed her mother could hide with four other kittens following.

Soon, on those spindly legs, the cat started trying to scavenge food from the crew. They would laugh at her, toss her bits of ship's biscuits, watching her try to chew the hard bread. She couldn't tear the biscuits, so instead she would gnaw on them with teeth that were designed for tearing.

The first time she cornered a mouse, she was thrilled with the thought of such a big meal. But the little black mouse hadn't survived the rats and other cats easily. The cat cornered it, swiped a small paw full of small claws, catching the creature on the ear just enough to tear the skin. The mouse reared up, started squeaking loudly, and leapt, catching the cat in the nose and breaking the tender flesh. The mouse then chased the spindly legged cat around and up a barrel of salt meat. The cat was trapped for an hour while the mouse circled the barrel, squeaking triumphantly. Eventually, the cook coming in frightened the mouse away.

The cat was ashamed, and went back to hunting for bugs in the flour and oats, carefully avoiding the mouse.

As the days passed, Midna became more concerned for her safety. The crew started giving her hungry looks. They had been weeks at sea, and it was obvious that the crew were thinking about the pleasures they missed from shore. Lady Applewood took to hiding in her room as much as possible, but still had to emerge for meals. Captain Smoke insisted she could only eat in the galley, at his table, under the stares of the men. As often as she could, she would skip meals to stay hidden in her room.

Being hidden did make the voyage pass more slowly. She could only see the sun through a small porthole, which only opened a crack before jamming. She had learned that the hard way, when she tried to close it just before a heavy rain. The afternoon had been hot and humid, even on the ocean, but a chilly wind came up suddenly that evening, and she could not get the porthole to close. It was getting dark and she knew, with the weather, the captain would not spare anyone to help with her problem. She slept with the window open, buried under all of her blankets and dresses to keep away the damp cold. The next morning at breakfast, she asked the captain if he could fix her window, and he sent down his second officer, who made comments about her attire and how solitary her room was while he closed the window.

From then on, she refused to open her window, and would push her heavy trunk in front of her door when she retired after supper.

One morning, Captain Smoke announced to the crew over breakfast, "It's high time we find some land. We're half a day from Bridgetown. What say you all to a few days of fun and relaxation?" He dragged the last word out while the crew cheered, everyone knowing that relaxation would be the last thing on their minds.

The crew hooted and hollered, excited for a few days of shore leave. The captain gave them a moment, then told them to talk to the first mate about leave rotations, and called on a few specific individuals to start inventorying what supplies were needed.

The captain sat back town and leaned toward Midna. "Now," he spoke softly to her, "don't you worry your pretty little head about finding things to do on shore. You know I won't be letting you off this ship. Can't have ya' running away or trying to find some high noble plantation owner who might send word to your family, now can I? No, I think you'll stay right where you are." He grinned his wicked grin. "But at least the men will burn off some of that extra energy. Maybe you'll even consider not barring your door for a while."

He laughed heartily as she blushed.

"I was only trying to protect myself, Captain."

"But from who?" He put on a posh accent, "All of my men are high quality, upstanding gentlemen who would never think of harming a hair on the head of a find Lady such as yourself."

She shuddered. "No, of course not, Captain. I would never presume…"

He leaned back and laughed. A full belly laugh that caused many of the crew to stop, food partway to their mouths, and watch. After a minute, the crew resumed eating and the captain wiped tears from his eyes, still chuckling.

"*I* am what keeps them out of your room, and no trunk would stop them if I gave the word." He leaned close again. "But you will find that while they are on shore you will be able to move more freely around the deck. Get out of that stuffy room."

"Thank you, Captain."

"And just to show you that I am not an evil man, perhaps I will pick you up some proper boots for the deck. Without your fancy boots you'll have no excuse to hide in your room all day." That wicked grin again. "And if you are lucky, I'll make contact with your family to see if they will meet the ransom demands."

She bowed her head, careful to keep her fear out of her words. "Thank you, Captain. You are too generous." Most of all, she feared his optimism that there would be a ransom.

The captain laughed again, before turning back to his meal.

The cat hunted and grew. From the small flies that swarmed the fruit after the first day or two at sea, the cat moved on to pill bugs in the flour, then the cockroaches in the oats. The big ones hissed, and she had trouble getting her claws through their shells, but once she figured out that when flipped, their undersides were soft, they were an easy meal. She enjoyed how they crunched. Anytime the boat stopped and more food came on board, the large flies that flew lazily around made for a great adventure. The cat would jump and climb until she would get close enough to leap, catching the creature in her mouth, and popping it between her teeth before she hit the ground. She learned that if you left the spiders alone, they would get bigger and bigger until they were a satisfying snack; better if she could avoid getting the sticky web on her paws or face.

The insects were good, but she was growing and needed more. Her legs were growing stronger. She could jump higher and land without hurting her paws. Her claws were longer and more dangerous, able to shred the bags of flour and bugs. Her fur grew in soft and full, a thick protection around some of the more delicate areas.

As she grew, the cat thought often of the mouse. The little black one. With all of her growing, there was still a little divot in her nose from where that mouse had bitten. She decided to brave that corner of storeroom again, just to see if the mouse was still there. After all, she had eaten all of the bugs she could find, and she was hungry again.

Sneaking, the cat walked into the room. It was mostly empty, the ship having been on the waves for weeks. She knew the mice liked the corners, while the rats liked the lower deck where it was dark and damp. She circled a barrel, sniffing it. It didn't smell like salt and meat, so it couldn't be the same one from the last time she saw the mouse. She crept from the shadow of the barrel and saw a flicker of movement. Hunkering down, she lashed her tail out to the side, flicking it slightly in the light. The small creature saw the movement and froze. The cat flicked again, and watched the mouse. It had a tear in its ear, but it couldn't be the same mouse as before, it was much smaller with some grey around its nose. The mouse she knew was big, black as the shadows, and terrifying.

The mouse started to move, and the cat flicked her tail again, freezing it in place. She pounced, claws out, and pinned the creature. It hardly had a chance to move. She looked at it more closely, shivering under her paw. Could it really be the same mouse? Had she grown so much? Her claws were now longer and sharper, her milk teeth replaced by strong fangs, and she had grown. How had she been so afraid of this little mouse? She pulled back her free paw, and gave the mouse a strong swipe, knocking its head so hard that she heard a faint crack and it stopped shivering. It somehow seemed uneventful, but made for a very satisfying meal.

With the crew off on shore leave, Midna felt safer wandering the deck. Only two pirates remained on board, stationed at the gangplank to make sure she did not leave nor anyone else come aboard. Neither were happy to have the duty, so she gave them a wide berth. She wandered the deck, enjoying the sun and the fresh air. Her cabin had become so stuffy, and it was nice to feel the warmth of the sun. But her goals were more than a little sun. She had smuggled some whitefish from supper and kippers from breakfast. Each were wrapped in silk handkerchiefs (she did have a slight pang knowing they would never come clean) and hidden in the folds of her skirt. She wanted to meet this cat that had everyone so afraid.

She kept her eyes to the masts, watching for movement.

After a bit, she saw a seagull land on the mid-mast. She moved under it, and sat on the deck, watching. Moments later, she saw the cat, leaping gracefully, closer and closer to the gull. As the cat approached, it slowed, crouched, and lashed its tail, distracting the bird. In a flash, the cat made what looked to be an impossible jump, grabbed the gull by the neck, and gave it a jerk. The gull did not even have a chance to flap its wings before it was all over. The cat trotted back with its meal. It walked the masts with no more difficulty than if it were on solid land.

Midna was amazed, and understood why the pirates were so afraid of the little beast. She slowly removed her purloined fish, crawling a little forward to spread one handkerchief out, the whitefish, then sat back so it was out of reach. She stretched, and put the stronger smelling kippers at the end of her reach. She sat, waited, and hoped.

After what must have been a couple of hours, the sun having moved past the apex, indicating her own lunch had passed, she saw a movement in the rigging closest to the further handkerchief. The cat was sniffing around. Midna kept herself as still as possible, lest she frighten the creature away. It hopped on the deck, sniffed some more, looked straight at her, and walked to the whitefish, gave it one more sniff, then ate. Once done, the cat sat and looked at Midna. She wondered if the cat had ever had many dealings with people, especially now that they were all so afraid of it. Midna hummed quietly, trying to make a gentle noise that wouldn't frighten the creature, but perhaps comfort it. The cat's ears flattened at the sound, and it crouched, watching Midna, but after a minute, it raised itself, and started to walk forward.

Suddenly, the cat's ears flicked, and it turned and ran, climbing the mast and disappearing. Not a second later, Midna heard the sounds of boots on the gangplank. She scooped up the kippers and the other handkerchief, tucked them into her pockets, and ran to her cabin, in case it was not the captain, but other crew returning.

Once safely back in her cabin, or as safely as she could be on this ship, she sat on her bed. The cat didn't seem too bad. It was certainly a killer, but it did not seem mean. She opened her porthole. It they were going to be in port for a few days, she could let the air in, and, opening the package of kippers and placing it on the desk under the window, perhaps more. She busied herself by trying to clean the other handkerchief in her washbasin, and waited for the captain to call her to supper.

After the mouse, the cat was much braver, willing to go after not just the mice that came on with fresh shipments, but the rats who always seemed to be on board. They were bigger, and more aggressive, and sometimes put up a fight, but other times, she played with them, letting them think they could get away, before she pounced. The other cats, who had once isolated her as the runt, now avoided her for another reason. The ship was now her territory, and she confined them to the kitchen, where they could hunt, but also had to avoid the cook's knives. Every time they came to land, more of the other cats left for better hunting grounds. Soon, the ship was hers.

She still didn't know what to do about the humans.

They no longer threw ship's biscuits at her, but now sometimes threw boots, tin cups, or even knives. She avoided the humans, and stayed mainly in the larder until on one long voyage between visits to land, the larder was almost empty and the rats were all gone. She ventured up to the deck, looking for something to eat.

The deck was bright, and the shadows were few and far between. She slinked along the edge of the gunwales, scurrying from shadow to shadow, searching for something to hunt. She heard a bang and flattened, running faster to the next shadow. Another bang. She reached the shadow and looked around. Two of the men were looking up and shooting at something. She had never heard the guns so close; most fighting took place on the deck while she was safely in the larder. One of them fired again, then both cheered. Something fell from the sky, thumping heavily close to the cat. She looked at it, then looked at the men. They were ignoring it, again looking to the sky, perhaps for other things to shoot.

The cat leapt forward, grabbed the thing in her teeth, and dragged it back to the shadow. It wasn't furry like the mice and rats. The outside was soft under her teeth, but at the same time there was something stiff in the softness. She dropped it, and used her nose to spread it out. A bird. She bit the edge of one wing, and sneezed as a bit of feather tickled her nose. It seemed to be all bone underneath anyway. She sniffed the middle of it, all around the belly and up the throat. She sniffed where the bullet had killed it, and sniffed the red around the feathers. She poked it with her paw, then bit. It was delicious. So rich and oily, and so very different from the rodents. Now this was good food. She would have to learn how to get more of this.

Lady Applewood was dozing on her bed when someone banged on her door, startling her.

"Cap'n wants you up for supper. He seys you got five minnuts," came a gruff voice, followed by retreating boot heels.

She got up, straightened her skirts and fixed her hair. She rearranged the desk, so that if anyone opened the door, they would not see the kippers so clearly placed under the porthole. A couple of books stacked in front would do. She also grabbed her cleaner handkerchief, though it still smelled a little of fish.

At supper, she took her usual seat next to the captain. Captain Smoke grinned at her. "I sent a Marconi to your father. I expect we'll be in port for a day or two, so he had better reply. In the meantime, I picked up something for ya'. Don't worry, I'll add the cost to your ransom!" He laughed as he pointed to a couple of parcels next to her seat. She lifted the lids of each and saw boots and what looked to be men's clothing. His grin grew larger. "Now you'll be able to walk the decks freely, without worrying about skirts and slippers. No more hiding in the room." He laughed again.

She wanted to cry. She wanted to yell. She wanted his heart on a platter. But all she said was, "Thank you, you are too kind;" and did her best to meekly smile at him. She was so tired of this song and dance.

When the food came, it was fresh beef, a real treat after being at sea for so long. She waited until the captain started to ignore her, cut away a large piece and slipped it into her handkerchief. When he next glanced over, he noticed how much food was gone.

"Hungry?" he asked.

"I had no lunch, not even a biscuit at midday."

He looked her over and nodded. "If I'm to get a good price, I can't have ya' go hungry. Take extra at breakfast. There'll be no lunch while we're in port. The men and myself would rather eat on shore."

"Thank you again," she said. "You do treat me well, considering."

He glared, and she regretted that last word. But then he grunted, and went back to his meal. She ate quickly and returned to her room, balancing her packages. The first thing she noticed was that the kippers were gone.

The next morning, she wore her new clothing to breakfast. The boots were too wide, but she ripped up one of her underskirts and wrapped her feet to fill the space. The britches were a little big, but she could cinch the belt. The shirt was tight across her chest. She opted to wear her corset over it, to better hide herself. No one would mistake her for a male, so she might as well keep some comfort. In fact, it was more comfortable because she had not been able to tighten her corset sufficiently over her smallclothes, and was always worried about her movement. The tight shirt between her smallclothes and corset gave her more freedom of movement, as did the britches for that matter. This perhaps was not what the captain had in mind, but she rather liked it.

The beef she had put out overnight was still on the

desk. She left it, hoping the cat would come back for it, but knowing it might be an unusual smell to a creature used to rodents, fish, and birds. After all, a ship like this would only have fresh beef when in port and for a day or two after.

She left the room for breakfast, armed with permission to take extra food.

Catching birds was not easy. The rigging was easy to climb. The cat could dig her claws into the hemp and propel herself in any direction with a spring of her hind legs. The masts, on the other hand, were covered in something and would get oily and slippery when wet, and sticky when it was hot. She learned how to keep her balance as they narrowed, and how to climb up and down the main masts. She learned the best routes to take, and how to navigate when the sails were up. This was much better than skulking in the dark. It was also much better than when she tried to take fish from the water. She did not mind the rain, but she did not like the salt ocean in her fur.

She enjoyed the sun. When not hunting, she would find a perch and lie out. She learned the men could only go certain places, so she would pick one away from the rigging where they could not reach, and would lie out, belly exposed, warming her fur.

She also found the birds were not expecting danger. They were used to dominating the tops of ships, and unless someone shot them, they were safe. They also had very little defence. They could bite, and their feet had claws, but some of the larger rats were scarier. She found, as long as she was quiet, if she could get in pouncing range, the birds did not stand a chance.

She still hunted the mice and rats. She no longer wanted to, but found that when she didn't, they brought more cats on board. If she cleaned out the rodents, she did not have to deal with other cats. This was her territory. She also became less fearful of the men. For the most part, they left her alone, but some nights, when the ship was at land, and the men returned swaying and singing, they would do things like throw rocks at her, or once, even tried to shoot her. Only once. The man who fired a gun at her lost his eyes to her claws. With a cry that would put a banshee to shame, she had leapt from the lower part of the mast, a fall that would likely kill her, but she had a soft target. With her claws out, she had landed on his face and slashed at his eyes with her forepaws, and dug in to his shoulders with her back claws. After the eyes, she dug her foreclaws into the side of his head and was about to bite his nose when two other men pulled her off. She scampered back up the rigging, hissing and screeching as she went.

She never saw the man with the gun after that, and the others left her alone to hunt.

Once the crew, save two, were gone, Midna went on deck and again looked for the cat. The beef was gone when she returned from breakfast, and she had fresh flying fish from breakfast. She had forgotten how much she missed fresh food after being on a ship so long. There had also been fruit and bread. She had taken some extra bread, an apple, and some fish. The captain watched, but said nothing. She knew he was keeping a tally, imagining how much money he could ask for. She also knew time was short. He would get a reply today or tomorrow, if her father even took the time to reply. She doubted he would. The Queen had changed the terms of inheritance and as the oldest the title would be hers, something her father could not allow. He was determined that the title and land would go to her brother, as centuries of tradition dictated. So he had sent her away. He said it was to learn about the world before taking over the lands, but she knew he hoped she would never return. One did not send a lady to the colonies without any escorts and expect her to return home with her honour intact, if she managed to return home at all. Now these pirates were making it easier for him. If he ignored them, they would kill her, but only after they made sure there was nothing left to her honour. If he answered, she hoped the best case would be that Captain Smoke would kill her in a fit of rage.

She really did not like either option.

Lost in thought, she had not noticed that the cat had come down, and was eating the fish. Startled, she shifted unconsciously. The cat froze, looked at her, and went back to eating. She took a chance and broke off a piece of bread for herself. The cat, rather than run, came forward, slowly, with its nose in the air. Looking at it, she broke off some more bread, and tossed it toward the cat, who sniffed at it, then ate it! She broke off another piece, and held it forward, leaning just a little. The cat came forward, sniffed, and took it from her fingers. Settling back, she tried for one more, breaking more bread, and holding it next to her. Once again, the cat came forward and ate it. Knowing the risk, she had heard the stories from the captain, she lifted her hand. The cat froze, looked at the hand and looked at her, then straightened up, bopping its head off the underside of her hand.

Midna was thrilled. She did not think she could have gotten so far so quickly. Captain Smoke was full of stories of this murderous cat, but really, it seemed to want affection. She scratched behind the cat's ear, and it actually purred.

Like the day previous, the cat froze, then ran off moments before Midna heard anything. This time, it wasn't heavy boots on the gangplank, but lighter shoes and higher voices. Women. From what she could make out, women were propositioning the two pirates on guard. Midna crept closer and could see three women, giggling and touching the two men. One of the pirates fumbled a coin from his pocket, tossed it in the air, caught it, and cursed. The other smiled and walked away with one of the ladies of pleasure.

A few minutes later, one of the women wandered away, the pirate's attention fully on the other. She spotted Midna, and started to turn away, when Midna gave a little wave. If this worked out, she would need people.

That evening, Captain Smoke was angry. There had been no message yet. While at sea, time seemed infinite, but on shore, they ran the risk of meeting the Queen's Guard or the local police force. He had expected that it would take two days for a reply, but did not like the reality of it.

Throughout supper he wavered from taunting her to asking her why there had not been a response. She mollified him as much as possible, but his temper was fearsome. He threatened her, as if she could make the message arrive faster. She tried to stay passive, meek, and show fear where she felt he wanted it. She was so sick of acting.

At least the mutton was good. And the pockets in her new britches allowed her take to take a larger piece for the cat. She also walked out of the galley with a mug of fresh milk.

The cat was in her room when she opened the door. Strange, it seemed this fearsome creature just wanted companionship. She offered the cat the milk, and it drank happily. She shredded the mutton with her fingers and put in on the handkerchief. The cat ate while she rubbed its soft fur.

She spoke softly to the cat, "You are a nice kitty, aren't you? I wonder if you will help me."

The cat looked at her, and Midna took that as a positive sign. "Who are you, kitty?" she asked quietly. "Puss? Fluffybottom? The Golden Blur Among the Masts? She Who Licks the Marrow from Your Bones?"

The cat bopped her head up at that last one, pressing against Midna's hand.

"She Who Licks the Marrow from Your Bones. That's another good sign, I hope. So, Marrow, I think we may need to take over the ship tomorrow. What do you think about that?"

Marrow looked at her with big, green eyes, then went back to her meal.

The cat liked this one. There had been something missing in her life, and this woman showed her what it was. The men had always been mean and never tried to give her good food or touch her. They gave her ship's biscuits, and threw things at her. They yelled and stomped. This one was different. This one was nice, and she enjoyed having her fur touched: it was like the warm sun, but better. She really enjoyed having her ear scratched.

She wanted this one to stay on her ship.

The next day, Captain Smoke came back at midday. He threw open the door to Midna's room. It was empty. He turned, and came face to face with the cat. Captain Smoke stepped back, and saw that the cat was on Midna's shoulder.

"Captain, whatever might be the problem?" asked Lady Applewood.

"The cat! How? The cat?" he stammered and collected himself. Forcing himself to look away from the cat to her, he tried to glare. "I've word from Lord Applewood. He refuses the ransom. I've spent too much time and effort with you, and he won't send a thing!" The captain started to raise his gun, but stopped when the cat started to growl.

"Yes, I am actually surprised he even answered," Midna replied in her best parlour room conversational tone. "You see, he would rather see me dead so that my brother will inherit." She said this so matter of fact that it took a moment for him to realise what she said.

"Ya' knew I'd get nothing! And ya' said nothin'!" he started to raise his voice.

"Of course I said nothing, silly man." She turned her back on him, but the cat shifted and continued to stare. "You would have killed me in an instant. Or worse, given me to your men, which you are always so quick to threaten." She started to walk out of the hall to the deck when Marrow leapt from her shoulder. She turned to see that Captain Smoke had once again raised his gun, but stopped aiming it at her as the cat flew at him. He tried to guard his face, but when he moved his hand to his face, the cat attacked his throat. When he moved his hands down, Marrow went for his face. The cat was merciless, and did not stop clawing until the pirate captain was on the ground and still.

Midna stepped forward, offering Marrow a shoulder as she picked up Captain Smoke's gun. She had never used a pistol before, but believed the basics were close enough to a hunting rifle that she could make do. Besides, she may not even need the gun for anything more than show. She had She Who Licks the Marrow from Your Bones, who had settled on her shoulder and started to clean the blood from her paws.

Gun in hand and Marrow on her shoulder, Lady Applewood, heir to the largest estate in the empire, after those controlled by the Queen herself, raised one foot and kicked the door to the deck open in a very unladylike manner. The crew present turned to look at her. Most were still in port, but she would never have been able to handle a dozen crew on her own.

"Captain Smoke is dead!" she spoke loud and clear,

making sure everyone present could hear every word. "This ship now belongs to me, and if anyone objects, they can take it up with Marrow here."

At her name, Marrow leaned over and nuzzled the side of Midna's face. She wanted to smile at the affection, but this was not over.

"An' what makes ye t'ink we'll sail under a woman?" The first mate spat the last word and stepped toward her.

Marrow tensed, and pounced. The first mate shrieked as the cat flew at his face, clawing for his eyes. Marrow remembered this man. He liked to stomp at her and had caught the tip of her tail a couple of time under his heavy boot.

As he screamed, Midna answered, addressing the gathered pirates who started frozen by the attack: "I do not think any of you will sail under a woman. So, you will all leave. It would be best for you to all just turn around and walk off of the ship. This is my ship now," she re-stated.

At this, footsteps ran up the gangplank. At least twenty women appeared, dressed much like Midna in britches, shirts, and corsets. Many wore men's tricornered hats and carried weapons.

Lady Applewood continued, "I do not need you to crew my ship, for my crew has arrived. Take that man," she indicated the former first mate who was curled on the deck, clutching his face, Marrow stepping back but growling at the men, "and remove yourselves from *my ship*!" She said the last two words as loud as she could, and the women erupted into cheers.

The men glared, but as Marrow took up her place on Lady Applewood's shoulder, no one was brave enough to attack. A couple of them helped the first mate up, and they filed down the gangplank and off the ship.

One of the women approached Lady Applewood, now captain of the ship. "Ma'am, Captain, there are a few more women gathering their things. They should be here within the hour."

"Excellent," replied Midna. "And your name?"

"Felicia. I was madam of the brothel, but myself and all of the girls agreed that your proposal was much better than having to put up with these ruffians for another day."

"I understand. How would you like to be my first mate?"

"Honoured. Some of the women have some ship experience. Some have even passed as men to gain passage to the colonies, looking for better lives and all. Most would have been better off in the poverty they left to this life…" Felicia mused, but brightened up. "Where will we be going next?"

"I haven't decided, but once we are all on board, I am open to suggestions. For now, I will be moving my possessions from my old room to my new rooms, ones better suited for the captain of the ship. I will put you in charge of deciding tasks and bunking arrangements. Oh, and if someone could toss the former Captain Smoke overboard, I would be quite thankful."

"Consider it done," replied First Mate Felicia with a curtsey that clearly showed respect, but would never have passed in polite society. Midna loved it.

Lady Applewood turned and walked away, Marrow perched on her shoulder. Wherever they went, she would be sure to send word to her father that she was still alive.

Jennifer Shelby

Jennifer Shelby hunts for stories in the beetled undergrowth of New Brunswick's fairy-infested forests. She fishes for them in the dark space between the stars. These stories, and many others, are made available through her catch-and-release program. You can learn more at jenni-fershelby.ca or on twitter @jenniferdshelby.

In 2021 she released her first novella, *Plague of the Dreamless: A Slipstreamers Adventure*.

Stormslayer

The mermaid's pinky and ring finger were gone, her middle finger halved at the knuckle, the webbing between it and her forefinger torn. This tear refused to heal. The hurt it caused had become a sacred echo of the pain in her heart for the child she lost in the same accident, but one finger and a thumb were enough to twist the lid of her glass jar and seal a thunderstorm inside.

Lightning flashed, angry at its capture. It wanted to be free, to thunder and growl and smash rain upon everything. "You must be patient, for I am Stormslayer and I have plans for you," the mermaid told the storm.

In the golden age of merfolk, a mermaid could conjure a hurricane with her wrath. In the modern age, the oceans were sick and microplastics weighed down its magic. A sudden thundershower was the best she could manage, but what Stormslayer lacked in power she intended to make up for in patience.

Her storm stowed, she dove into the Bay's deepest channel to pick her way past piles of abandoned netting, broken traps, and other debris. The thick silt of the Bay made secrets of ships until they were upon her. She'd learned well to keep to this channel.

Her missing fingers twitched with ghosts, forever untangling her daughter's hair from the boat propellor that killed her. Stormslayer had cut her own locks short as soon as she was able.

A cave lay ahead in the muddied gloom. A hagfish grinned and swished past, its movements enough to shift the silt gathering on a net filled with Stormslayer's jars. Each one contained a storm that boiled with impatience. Stormslayer shifted the net and added the new storm, gentle with the glass. The storms ached for release, to race to the surface and explode over the Bay, to barrel into the houses of the humans who stole her daughter's body and scoured the Bay for more mer-kind. Stormslayer had been helpless then, recovering from her own near-fatal wounds. She wasn't any longer.

Leaving the cave, she paused and listened for the echoes of the sea, the bright spark of snapping claws, the shush of shifting seaweeds, and for the deadly rhythmic hum of motors. The tide pulled at her tail as it emptied from the Bay. There would be few boats until the tide turned, the water too shallow and seafloor too jagged with rocks. A dangerous urge tugged at her scarred body, stronger than the tides. It was a hopeless quest, a mother's quest, and a mermaid's habit to check the ring of debris along the shore for news of friends, foes, and warnings of pollutants. Maybe the humans had finally returned her daughter from wherever they took her after they dislodged the propellor from her skull. Her body should have been fed back to the fishes, setting the child's soul free to swim the vastness of the oceans.

Close to the shore now, uneven splashes made Stormslayer cautious. She rose to see what creature made them, her head low, the nictating lens that protected her from the silt sliding open across her large, seal-like eyes. A juvenile human, a child, splashed on the beach. The child had stripped down to its underwear, its torso rippled with dark bruises, ribs and bones poking out from its skin.

Stormslayer watched and soon understood that the child was trying to catch a fish, though this made no sense. The best fish swam in deeper water; these sandy shallows better for digging clams. Little wonder the creature appeared to be starving.

It wasn't safe to linger in this place where the boat with the open propellor stalked the sea. The mermaid sensed nothing but driftwood, a few shells, some kelp, and the leg bone of a deer in the tidal debris. She should have gone, but the mother she once was kept her close. Human children often drowned, and this child should not have been left to play here without supervision.

The mermaid watched the child. A girl, she supposed seven-years-old, her hair dangerously long and knotted. Only when the girl abandoned the beach did Stormslayer leave.

She moved to the open sea to sleep, upright like a whale, but she returned to the cove the following day. The child was there again, this time with a stick, string, hook, and a bit of seaweed for bait. The gurgles of her empty stomach carried along the water. Her movements had grown sluggish, but her expression remained determined.

Stormslayer didn't like to see the fresh, purpled bruise

on the child's cheek. The mermaid had watched many humans from the safety of the sea. They tended to treasure their offspring, as Stormslayer had her daughter, yet this child was bruised and left unfed. This place must be as cursed as she suspected. First to murder her daughter, steal her body, and now to leave a child to fend for herself.

The mermaid searched along the seafloor until she located a blue crab. She stung it with the barb hidden in her fluke. Mermaid venom was swift to kill and quick to become inert, useful for a merciful death to a small creature or an escape from a larger one.

Stormslayer scooped up the crab with her damaged hand and turned back to the shore. She approached the child with care to keep the sun behind her to hide her true form. The girl's eyes were wary and her body still with fright when Stormslayer held out the food. A moment of hesitation dissolved into a quick snatch of the meal and a retreat to the beach. The child smashed open the shell with a rock and gulped at the meat.

Stormslayer slipped beneath the waves and returned with a large rockfish, daring to show her hand this time as the girl took the fish. Less desperate now, the child's attention lingered on Stormslayer's palm. Her gaze met the mermaid's. "You're not a seal," the child whispered.

Words sounded strange in the air, but Stormslayer had been taught well in her pod days. The mermaid chose not to speak, yet rose from the water to show her face and her shoulders before she dove and swam far away.

Her heart burned. It was a brazen, foolish thing she'd done, to reveal herself to a human. No good could come of this. How many merfolk had been tempted by humans, only to be lured into treacherous tidepools and trapped, never to swim again? But surely a child would not hold such malice, such a lack of wonder.

Concern for the girl drew Stormslayer back to the cove after the tide filled and emptied twice. The child scanned the water, hands clasped in a desperate hope.

The mermaid saw relief shift the child's posture when she spotted her, the brightness in her expression when the girl reached for the large bass Stormslayer brought from the open sea. The child didn't devour it this time. Instead, she did a strange thing, awakening a bright, dancing being on the edge of a stick. She held it to a bundle of paper and twigs. The dancer grew, its body an orange, flickering light that blackened the wood and curled into a stinking fog that rose to join the sky. Stormslayer moved closer, fascinated by this dancer, as the girl set the fish upon a dented bit of metal.

The fire crackled, snapped, and startled the mermaid. The smell, the sound, the sight of it! She must touch it; she must know this thing. Stormslayer crawled from the water and reached for the flames. The girl gasped as she took in the terrible scar where the propellor had cut off Stormslayer's left breast and dug deep into her ribs, the iridescent scales of her tail, and her beautiful green fluke.

Stormslayer readied to plunge her hands into the fire and snatch the dancing creature. "No! Be careful, it's hot!" shouted the child, the fright in her voice enough to stay Stormslayer's hand. Once delayed, the mermaid felt the heat the strange dancer made and drew her hand back, more fascinated still.

"It's fire," said the girl. "It eats air and wood to cook meat, but water puts it out." The girl put her hand in the Bay and flicked droplets into the flames. Stormslayer giggled to hear them sizzle.

"My name is Naia." She knelt before the mermaid. "Can you understand me?"

Stormslayer drew herself up, leaning on her elbows. "I am Stormslayer and I understand you."

Naia's mouth fell open and stayed there a long moment before she closed it. "Do you actually slay storms?"

Stormslayer cocked her head to the side and did not tell the girl she planned to slay *with* storms. Such ideas were not for children.

"Thank you for the fish." The child tried to smile, only to wince when it reached her bruised cheek.

"Why is there none but a mermaid such as I to feed you?"

Naia said nothing, her body folding itself smaller. Her hands clutched one another, knuckles white.

"There are blossoms of the bruise scattered over your skin that whisper of unkind acts. Should I worry for you, child?" Stormslayer asked.

Naia stared at the sand. Someone had made the girl afraid to say anything. Stormslayer sighed and pushed herself into the water, the sea's cool embrace a relief from the hot and cloying air. She could smell the dancing fire on her skin, and she wasn't sure she liked it.

A tiny hole burrowed into the sand drew Stormslayer's attention. "Come, behold this small darkness," she told the girl.

Naia stepped over and peered into the hole. "Follow this darkness into the sand and it will lead to food." Stormslayer dug with both hands to reveal the clam hidden underneath. She passed it to Naia, who added the clam to her fire, but the fish had begun to reek and mingle with the dancing fire's stink. Stormslayer's nostrils burned and her stomach twisted at its strangeness. "I will leave now, Naia."

"No, wait! Will I see you again?" There were several notes of desperation in the girl's voice.

The mermaid slipped her face under the water to cleanse her senses and resurfaced. "I will come to you again."

Stormslayer did, too, the following day, cursing her heart for slipping so easily in love with a human. She'd once paid heed to a hundred similar stories in her pod, each of them ending badly for the mer. Stormslayer had chosen to spend her mourning time alone, and now her pod was too far to see her folly or warn her away with their disapproval. Everything flowed together to allow her relationship with the child to deepen, just like in the stories, but she couldn't help herself.

The sun sat high and hot, Naia's now-familiar form nowhere Stormslayer could see. She stayed in the water and listened for the girl. Perhaps the child had found a proper mother to look after her. The thought of it ignited a fierce jealousy in Stormslayer's heart. She'd wait, to be sure, and rested in the cool, silty waves, while she drifted closer to a small dock.

Stormslayer had seen enough of the structures to know the humans used them to hold their boats. It fascinated Stormslayer with its nonsense: constructed of tree ripped from the land, stripped of their leaves and their life, only to be shoved down into the earth again beneath the sea, all to make a place to step from land to sea without ever touching wet. She swam between the pilings and there, against a smash of broken barnacles — a streak of paint. Stormslayer stared at the precise shade of red which had haunted her nightmares for a year. The rhythm of a motor filled her mind. Her beloved's sharp shriek and the awful silence that followed. The red of the boat, the crimson water that swirled with blood. The mindless pain, those first few glimpses of human faces.

Stormslayer scraped her damaged hand and her ghost fingers along the sharp, broken barnacles. The sudden sting of salt and the bright spots of blood on her thumb and forefinger anchored her into the present, but her heart beat too fast, her eyes kept on seeing—

"Stormslayer!" a voice called on the wind. "Stormslayer, I'm here!" The child.

Naia ran into view, arms clutching a handful of white and green unknowns, cheeks rosy, a new bruise on her shoulder dark against a dirty yellow swimsuit.

Stormslayer pushed away from the piling and moved to the girl and the shore. Naia vibrated with excitement. "I brought you something." She displayed a bundle of land weeds with stems that leaked milk and wore caps of white fluff. "They're called dandelion clocks! You can blow on them and make wishes." Naia grabbed one, blew, and the fluffs swirled away like jellyfish larvae caught in a current. She handed one to Stormslayer. "You try."

Stormslayer puffed out a breath and the seeds plunged through the air. Others clung to her wet skin with soft, airy tickles and made the mermaid laugh.

Naia picked out the largest dandelion clock from her collection and handed it to Stormslayer. "Don't forget to make a wish."

Stormslayer blew a second whoosh of air. "I wish to know why you're here, alone with your bruises and your hunger, day after day."

The girl dropped her gaze to her lap. The mermaid caressed Naia's hand with the empty dandelion stem and sighed. "Perhaps these wishes do not come true."

"No! They do, they have to!" Naia clenched her fists and leapt to her feet. "Our parents died in a crash. My brothers look after me, so I don't have to go to a foster home or anything, but they're out fishing all day."

"It is they who cast these bruises over your flesh?" The waves whitecapped as Stormslayer's anger rose despite herself. She dug her fingertips deep into the sand to free the storm energy and calm herself.

The girl fiddled with her wishweeds, afraid to answer, but they told Stormslayer what she wanted to know. A breeze off the water sent a cloud of the wishes twirling around Naia's hunched form.

"What if I dragged you into the sea and made a mermaid of you?" The words slipped out unbidden, though Stormslayer felt their truth. "What if I pulled you down and filled your lungs with water? And what if I used my magic to grow your fluke and gills?" She crawled closer to the girl, her eyes fixed upon Naia's. "What if I taught you how to breathe down there with me? Undersea, you would be beloved of me, and the very waters will shift at your command, no longer prey to your human brothers.

Come with me and I will be your mother. All you have to do is drown."

Naia's mouth hung open, the whites of her teeth like pearls in an unshucked oyster. Her body trembled despite the warmth of the sun. Her eyes swam with a sudden wetness that made Stormslayer shift back into the water. The mermaid waved her hand, as if to swipe her words from the girl's memory. "This is a passing thought, I won't make a mermaid of you without your consent."

Naia found her voice at last. "I'd—I'd like to. I just… I need to think it over."

"Yes, think." Stormslayer flicked her tail, furious with herself and stung with hurt. Silly mer-heart to be so susceptible to humankind. She pushed herself back into the Bay, submerging to soothe herself before she faced the child again.

"Are you leaving?" Naia's face crumpled. "I hurt your feelings, didn't I? I'm sorry, it's just that drowning sounds like dying. Does it hurt?"

"I cannot say, I cannot drown," Stormslayer answered, fascinated to see water tumble in droplets from the girl's eyes. The mermaid reached out, caught a tear on her finger, and brought it to her lips. She gasped at the taste. "You have the sea inside you!" Little wonder humans stole merfolk hearts with such ease. Stormslayer leaned forward on her hands and kissed Naia's forehead. "I will wait until you are not afraid."

Naia smiled up at her. "You really want to be my mum?"

Stormslayer nodded. "You need a mother and I need a daughter. We are a match." She frowned as she looked at the girl's hair. "You must cut your hair short like my own to come with me. It isn't safe to keep it long."

Naia reached up and ran her hand through her hair, a crease of not-quite-understanding on her brow. "Okay. When I'm ready, I'll cut my hair."

The mermaid stared at the girl, seeing her mer-daughter's pretty tresses. How she loved to brush them, how fast they yanked her up into the human machine. The horror of her memories filled Stormslayer's mind and refused to stay quiet. "I must go."

The mermaid didn't return right away. A depression settled upon her like an algal bloom filtering out the light; she'd gone too deep inside of her worst memories. Her scars ached with their bitter ghosts and her daughter's death-scream echoed through the ocean. A day passed, and then another, before Stormslayer broke out of the prison her mind had created. Naia would be worried. Naia would be hungry.

Night had swallowed the sun and painted the sea with octopus ink. Stormslayer went to Naia's cove anyway, in the chance the girl might be there. She stopped to fetch a storm from her collection, a bright trinket to fill the girl with wonder.

The net of jarred storms looked full as the storms within glinted, lightning piercing through the dark and the silken silt. She had more than enough to rip out the coastline. It would already be gone if she hadn't met Naia. The thought reminded her of too many old pod tales to seem anything but ominous. Stormslayer pushed it away. She'd tell her own damn story.

A flicker of firelight shone through the water at Naia's

beach, but the figures around it were much larger than the girl. The familiarity of the voices slid a sludge of horror down Stormslayer's back and sent her searching for their boat. A red boat, its damaged propellor still open, bobbed at the dock. Stormslayer could smell the death upon it, see the mangled dent where the prop had bitten into a mermaid's skull. It had caught her beloved's long, trailing hair and pulled her up so fast.

A movement past the boat drew Stormslayer's eye. She could just make out Naia's form in the dark water. Stormslayer wedged her storm beneath a chunk of sunken wood and surfaced beside the child.

Naia's hair was shorn and Stormslayer's heart quickened with joy to see it. The girl needed a mother, Stormslayer needed someone to mother, and now they would be together.

Naia shook her head with urgency, her eyes full of fear. It was then that Stormslayer saw the boys had tied Naia to the piling, her face barely above the high-water mark.

"Come on, Little Bait," called one of the boys from the fire. "Tell us where the mermaid is and we'll split the profits with you."

"Yeah, right," said a second. A mean laugh scuttled over the water.

"Go," Naia mouthed.

Stormslayer didn't tell her she knew these brothers. The boys who did nothing to help and stole her daughter's body from the sea. The same boys who cruelly bruised her Naia, who left her to starve and to drown on the beach alone.

"It's a trap," Naia said in a whisper.

Of course it was, life always was, and stories with humans and mermaids were most definitely traps. But she was Stormslayer, hunted by sharks, stalked by orcas, and the humans who killed her first daughter and battered the next demanded no respect from her. Stormslayer dove, opening her fluke to its truest potential, heedless of any boats that might still stalk the Bay. She didn't slow until she arrived at the mouth of the cave and pulled her treasure free.

She piled her storms on the sea floor along Naia's beach. The boys guffawed at their fire while Naia wept beneath the pier. Stormslayer crept close to the shoreline, daring the boys to spot her, but the firelight dimmed their eyes. She stole a large stone from the shore.

A boy looked out, unseeing, as she hammered the stone into her jars. The water muffled the smash of the glass. The storms bubbled to the surface, raging with freedom and the power they held in each other.

Flashes of lightning and a growling thunder shuddered over the cove. The water heaved with fury. Stormslayer went for the boat first. She pulled it down and rent it in two, wood and fiberglass splintering beneath the anger of her ghost fingers. Her magic struck the propellor and disintegrated the metal into rusty flakes that washed into the sand and with them something broke, inside her and without. The world grew narrow and quiet as her daughter settled into peace at last.

Stormslayer dared not linger in the moment, for Naia, still tied to the piling, needed her. The waves crested over the girl's head as she fought to breathe. Stormslayer fumbled with the knots, but they were well tied, and her ghost fingers could find no purchase to help. Naia's time ran short and suddenly the knots were her mer-daughter's night-black hair tangled in a prop Stormslayer couldn't pull free. She tried to hold back the propellor's blade with her hand, but it sliced past her fingers, into her breast, and — the ropes gave, weakened by the smashed barnacles beneath them, freeing Naia.

Stormslayer helped her keep her face above wild waves, wincing as Naia sputtered and coughed the sea from the lungs. The mermaid carried her to the shore on the far side of the pier. "Climb quick and high where the waves cannot snatch you."

Naia shook her head. Her teeth chattered in great spasms and her body shuddered. She clutched her arms together, tight to her chest. The storm winds whipped past her newly shorn head as thunder smashed the sky, dragging her attention upward. "No, I'm coming with you."

Stormslayer smiled, running her hand along the girl's scalp. "If I am to be your mother, you must listen." She turned to the pier. A dark figure stood on the dock, hunting for her by the light of lightning strikes. She didn't want to leave Naia, but the brothers would never stop and the next mermaid to happen upon the Bay must be protected. "Keep safe, Naia, I'll return for you."

The mermaid's stormsight showed the brother on the pier held a flare gun in his hands, another in his pocket. The second brother was in the water, attempting an ambush. He was a better swimmer than she'd expected from a human, however fatally foolish he must have been to stalk a mermaid in a storm of her own making.

She waited until the boy swam close enough to throw an arm around her neck to choke her. She let him do this, her gills unaffected by his methods, in hopes to find the answers she'd sought for a year. He whooped to the second boy who ran across the dock and aimed the flare gun into Stormslayer's face.

"Hey wait!" shouted the boy who held her. "The professor said we needed to bring this one in with her brain intact."

The boy with the gun sneered at Stormslayer. "Hear that? You're ours now."

"Yeah, ours like that hot little mermaid we got last summer," said the boy who held her. His tone held terrible secrets. Stormslayer's vision went bright with fury and the storm heaved as she flicked her fluke. The hidden barb lodged its venom into the boy's thigh.

His hold on her slackened, and she slipped into the dark sea, pulling the boy with her. She turned so he could see her watch him die in the lightning light, his face slack with shock.

The storm she'd stashed when she first arrived flashed with impatience through the gloom. Stormslayer swam for her jar. She wedged the boy's body under the driftwood and pulled the glass free.

"Jeremy!" The brother's voice had grown hoarse and frantic while she was underwater. Stormslayer watched from below the dock. "Where's my brother, you soggy bitch!" He stomped to the shore and grabbed a dark shape, jerking it upwards. Naia. The girl tried to curl up and protect herself as he aimed the gun at her. "Show yourself, you damn mermaid!"

Stormslayer illuminated the phosphorescence between the scales of her tail. "I am here."

"Where's Jeremy?" the boy hollered. He hauled Naia onto the dock and stormed toward the mermaid. "What did you do to him?"

"He is here," said Stormslayer. Her attention turned to Naia. "Dive." The girl broke away and plunged into the water as Stormslayer hurled the last storm at the brother. The boy flinched and fired the flare at the unknown missile in an explosion of chemical light.

Shattered glass rained on dock and sea alike. A bolt of lightning stretched with joy at its newfound freedom, catching the boy through his outstretched hand and zapping through his veins, past his heart, and down the femoral artery. It blew off his foot as it plunged into the old piling, buried deep into the earth beneath the shallows. He tumbled off the pier, into the Bay, and there the riptides claimed him.

Stormslayer lunged for Naia. She'd dove poorly and floated face down, a cut on her forehead spilling blood into the storm. The mermaid turned her over gently to help her breathe, but the girl did not respond. "Naia?" Stormslayer patted her cheek. "Naia!" She pressed her ear to the girl's chest, desperate to hear a heartbeat through the endless thunder of her storm.

"No, no, no, I will not lose you. I am Stormslayer and I will not let you die!" The mermaid roared, summoning power from the depths of herself and the sea, awakening a rage she thought long dead. As she gathered this magic, she worked it, Naia's body held tight against her own in a fierce embrace. Power swirled around them and into the girl. For hours Stormslayer wove this magic, and the storm raged.

Stormslayer awoke in a bright blue ocean. A deep weariness ached in her bones. She did not remember falling asleep. In her arms, she still clutched the human child, her magic all spent. She should let the girl go, allow the sea to have her, but she couldn't. At last, she understood the whales who clung to their dead calves for weeks after they'd passed.

Stormslayer should have listened to the pod stories. They might have saved Naia.

The sun streamed through the blue water in columns. A jellyfish floated above, a cruel reminder of Naia's wish-weeds. The ocean did not care about the wreckage of the mermaid's life.

The girl in her arms shifted. Stormslayer looked on, afraid to speak and break this spell. Naia's hands flew to her gills. She peered down at her fluke, a vibrant purple, and flicked, testing it out. When her eyes met Stormslayer's again, they were filled with wonder.

Stormslayer's heart thundered with pride and relief. "Come." She squeezed her daughter's hands. "I will take you to meet our pod. We have a new story to tell them."

Amanda Labonté

Amanda Labonté lives in St. John's, Newfoundland, where she gets much of the inspiration for the characters and places about which she writes. Though she knew she wanted to be a writer since the eighth grade, it was many years before she finally walked into a creative writing class and found a new home.

Her first novel, *Call of the Sea*, won critical acclaim in her home province of Newfoundland. The first book in her *Supernatural Causes* series gained Bestseller status on Amazon in September 2017.

As the co-owner of an educational business and mother of two, she spends much of her day with kids of all ages. They give her some of the best reading recommendations.

Regeneration

Strands of silver thread glinted in the last rays of sun as merrow in their human forms worked diligently on the pebbled beach.

Lia stood with her feet in the waves, her skirt catching a breeze and wafting out behind her. The merrow around her worked in pairs, their naked human legs stretched out in front of them as they focused on the task at hand. It was an activity she'd seen many times before, but never from the shore. She took a deep breath, filling her lungs with salty air. The cool water washing over her feet felt good and she fought the urge to walk further out.

She turned at the clunking sound of rocks shifting underfoot and watched as Annar approached, his six-foot figure moving gracefully over the stones. His blue eyes settled on her as he spoke.

"Nervous?"

She focused her attention back to the setting sun, on the pink and violet rays stretching out across the sky. Out of the corner of her eye she could see the outline of a young man, half in the water. He was tying off the end of a silver thread, his legs now firmly together. If Lia looked closely, she would probably see scales reforming.

But she didn't want to look.

"What's there to be nervous about?"

Annar reached out, taking her hand and giving her fingers a reassuring squeeze. "Your skin is cold."

"It's a cool evening."

"I think it's a sign you've been human too long."

Lia looked down at her feet, at her toes digging into the strip of sand at the water's edge. She could see the scarring — mostly faded now — from where the knife had cut her tail in half, letting her adopt a human form for the first time.

In her mind's eye, she could still see the flash of the silver, feel the cut of the blade against the scales of her tail. There'd been so much loss — blood, feeling, breath — she'd felt the horrifying sensation of smothering as her lungs had expelled water for air. She'd thought there was no possible way for her body to survive such a fundamental shift.

Then, almost before she realized it, she'd adjusted.

Her scales had been absorbed into milky skin forming legs. Soon, she'd been able to stand, run, even jump — the movements becoming as natural to her as swimming.

Well, almost as natural.

Annar shifted next to her, releasing her hand. "Are you ready?"

Lia blinked, the reality around her chasing away dreams of the past. The numbers on the shore were slowly diminishing as the merrow around her slipped into the waves.

"Is it possible to be ready?"

Annar's lips quirked up at the corner. "It isn't."

"But it gets easier?"

"It does, but not before it gets harder."

She repressed a snort. "You're not particularly comforting."

Annar appeared pensive for a moment before answering. "Would lies make you feel better?"

Lia watched as a sea bird glided above the waves, its wings a dark silhouette against the pink sunset. "I think, perhaps, yes."

"Like I said, you've been human too long."

Annar was right. Even as she watched the bird disappear behind a cliff, her body was hyper aware of the pull of the waves at her feet. She'd been avoiding the water more and more lately as she felt the call to return to the sea intensifying within her.

Still, she was going to miss the feeling of standing on land, eating dry food, experiencing a multitude of scents...

"It's not like it's forever," Annar's voice cut into her thoughts. "You will return."

"I know, but when?"

Of course he didn't answer. Lia hadn't expected him to.

There was a gentle splashing nearby as another merrow disappeared below the surface. Soon it would just be her and Annar left on shore.

"Here." His hand brushed against her arm to get her attention. He held a spool of fine silver thread out to her, the eye of a darning needle sticking out. She kept her hands firmly at her sides.

"You should go first."

Annar cocked his head to the side. "That's not how it works. I'm here to supervise in case…"

"In case it all goes wrong?"

"In case you require assistance."

The last of the merrow ducked into the water, leaving only Lia and Annar. The sun was fading fast. If they didn't work now, it would soon be too dark, and they'd have to wait another day.

She reached for the spool, the needle nicking her thumb. "Let's get started."

They settled on the sand, Lia fixed her skirt up around her thighs, sticking her bare legs straight out in front of her. She plucked at the needle, attempting to pull the thread through the eye, but her fingers were numb and she fumbled it. Finally, Annar took the needle, threading it one fluid movement before holding it out to her.

"The first few punctures are the worst. After that your body will adjust."

Lia nodded. Now that they were starting, she wasn't as scared. It would be all right. She took the needle, holding the point over the skin of her ankles. Just before she made the first stitch, she closed her eyes and focused on the face of the one person who would make this worth it.

Somewhere, not too far offshore, he was waiting for her.

Stacey Oakley

Stacey Oakley is an author originally from Moncton, New Brunswick who became a vibrant part of the local Newfoundland writing scene after the publication of "The Sorrows of War" in the 2016 edition of *Sci-Fi from the Rock*.

She has since gone on to independently publish her own novel, *Hunter's Soul*, its follow up *The Necromancer*, and in 2018 was crowned the winner of the 48 Hour Novel-Writing Marathon.

From the Depths

Sarah was at the harbour at dawn, watching the ships coming in, and waiting for one in particular. Maria's ship was supposed to be back any day now, and her lover had promised a long stay on shore before she and her crew left on their next adventure.

Maybe it would have been easier if Sarah would go as well, and she had, at one time. But almost drowning during a storm had left her with a healthy fear of the ocean, and what lurked beneath it, though she could never be certain if that had been a dream or not. Maria had been the one to pull her out of the water then, and nurse her back to health when the water wouldn't leave her lungs completely for some time after. So now she stayed on shore, a merchant selling the goods that Maria's crew brought back from around the world. Sometimes she envied them the stories of the lands they visited, the trials they faced, but she couldn't bring herself to go back to the water. She couldn't face the dark claws that tried to drag her into the depths of the ocean as her lungs filled with water.

She never begrudged Maria her need to wander. She was a creature of the sea at heart, trapped in human form.

She was as fierce and wild as any ocean storm, laughing where others would cower. She was a siren, luring others in with her songs. Sarah hadn't been able to resist it, but she'd never crashed upon the rocks for following it. Instead, it had brought her the deepest pleasure she'd ever known.

"No sign of 'em yet?" She looked back to see Tom O'Malley, one of the few shipwrights Maria trusted with *Ocean's Rose*, getting into his own small fishing boat. His nephew, a gangly youth whose name she couldn't remember, was lowering supplies into the boat from the dock. When she met his eyes, he quickly looked away, blushing.

"Not yet," she replied, turning her gaze back to the harbour and the ocean beyond.

"There were plenty 'o storms this year," he said. She understood the implication, but wholeheartedly rejected it.

"Maria's sailed through plenty of storms before," she reminded him without looking back. She didn't want to see his expression. "Worse than what we saw."

"The two of ye have been close for a long while, eh?"

"We have," she replied evenly. Since she'd run from a family that would never accept her at fifteen. Maria had found her in a bar, told her that looking into her eyes was like looking into the deepest ocean, and convinced her to sign onto the same ship. Maria had worked her way up the ranks, and into Sarah's heart, even after she was landbound.

"May the winds favour them," was all Tom said in the end before leaving with his nephew.

She'd heard some talk around town about her. Wealthy and powerful enough in her own right, well into her twenties and unmarried despite being a beauty. There had been plenty of suitors over the years who tried to court her, though most ran when they saw who she dealt with. She had no interest in marriage unless it was to her siren. But on land the church and the crown ruled, in that order. So, she would not be able to stand before all and declare her love for Maria. They had to keep it quiet, hidden from most. It had been one benefit of being at sea. The ocean didn't care who one loved, she treated them all the same, for better or worse.

The sun rose higher in the sky, cutting through the morning chill. Sarah knew it wouldn't be able to for long as autumn faded into winter. More fishermen readied their boats and left, largely ignoring her, especially as other women who awaited the return of husbands, lovers, sons, and fathers stood out on the docks, watching for sails on the horizon. Some prayed in quiet whispers, their heads bent over rosary beads that passed silently through their fingers. Watching the tiny crosses swaying in the winds, Sarah couldn't help but wonder if Mary really would pray for a sinner like her, or for Maria, who was named for her. Would she really believe they were in the wrong, even though their love was true? She couldn't believe this was some malevolent trick. It made her stronger, better as a person. She *wanted* to be better, to do the best she could, so that she deserved Maria's love. And Maria had said the same to her, many times over the years. It wasn't her fault that the King changed his mind so frequently on whether they were pirates or privateers.

The sun kept following its inexorable path through the sky, and Sarah had to move. She had to move, had work to do, and had to take care of herself. She sought out other arriving ships to find out where they'd been; if they'd crossed paths with *Ocean's Rose* or heard of others who had. The harbour wasn't near as large as those in the bigger cities in England and France, but it could fit a fair number of ships. It was especially popular among privateers when the crown declared them pirates.

At sunset she returned to the home she'd made for herself, a small house on the rise that overlooked the harbour and not far from the office she rented for work. She could have afforded something grander, but she preferred this, and it meant that fewer people asked questions about who she dealt with and what goods changed hands. Many were legitimate merchants and businesses, but quite a few were not. She had worked hard to gain their respect and had come to genuinely enjoy her work. Given that many ship captains approached her looking for assistance, it was a good thing, because she was often busy.

But not even work could take her mind off the worry. She had been confident then, but now threads of doubt crept into her mind. She knew Tom was right, there had been many storms. But Sarah knew that Maria and her crew had sailed through worse, and Roger, the first mate, was a good, steady hand who would probably become a captain himself one day. They were fine, just a little late.

Just before dawn, she rose and returned to the harbour, and stayed as long as she could, until work or other matters called her away. The same pattern repeated every day. The group of women that gathered changed with the days, some leaving the shore in joy, some in despair at waiting another night, and some in sorrow. But all who loved a sailor knew the risks. Each day, Sara moved closer and closer to the harbour, as if that would help her see the ships better, until she was physically standing on the docks, with only slats of wood between her and the gently rolling waves.

It was almost a month before she saw *Ocean's Rose* sailing into the harbour. It didn't take long before Sarah could see that the sails were ragged and worn, and the signs of hastily made repairs. Heart in her throat, she ran to meet the ship as it docked, and the crew began to disembark. They were in just as hard a shape, ragged and exhausted, salt-stained bandages visible through worn clothing. John, the cook, was lifted out on a stretcher. They still gathered around her with cheerful greetings, but the cheer didn't reach their eyes as they kept glancing back at the ship, waiting for something. They would only give her vague answers, and she started to get afraid. They'd be able to make the money to get the ship repaired, they hadn't been anywhere new, the seas had been rough, and they were all looking forward to being on land for a little while. That was all she could get out of them.

When Roger finally emerged and walked down the gangplank, the worry that had grown into terror over the past month didn't settle at all. When he met her eyes, she couldn't say what exactly gave it away. After all, the captain was the first to board, and the last to leave. Maria could have been taking care of any number of things just out of sight. She loved Sarah, but she had a duty to her ship and to her crew that she took very seriously. It was one of the reasons why Sarah had fallen in love with her.

But Sarah knew in that moment when her eyes met Roger's that Maria wouldn't be disembarking.

"What happened?" She struggled to keep her tone steady and failed, her voice cracking with emotion. Several of the crew looked away, but not before she caught how glassy their eyes were. Hardened sailors, many of them older than her, couldn't look her in the eye.

"The last storm… it was a ship breaker," Roger said, his voice soft and sorrowful. "One of the canons on deck came loose. She had to take herself off the safety line to get to it before it could cause more damage to the ship, or to the rest of us. She got it secured, but..." He trailed off, and Sarah didn't need him to finish.

"Maria was swept away."

"We tried to save her, or to find her." His voice broke, and he wiped away his tears before they could fall. "I'm sorry."

Sarah fell to her knees on the dock. Between the wooden slats, she could see the water moving, the ocean waves rolling and rippling across the surface, hiding so many secrets, holding so many sorrows.

Now hers was among them.

The ship and crew may have been Maria's, but Sarah was also close to them. So, she let them rest while she went in search of Tom to discuss repairs to the ship. To her good fortune, he was more than happy to handle them and get *Ocean's Rose* back in top form.

"I'm sorry for your loss," he said as Sarah signed the contract.

"Thank you." Her voice didn't waver, and she was proud of that. When she looked up from the paper, Tom was still looking at her.

"I heard an old legend, a myth, really, years ago about people lost at sea," he said, speaking in a low tone.

She raised a brow. "I didn't realize you were interested in those old stories." He had always seemed like the kind of man who needed proof to believe something. Though it shouldn't have been a surprise, Tom may not have been a sailor, but he'd been surrounded by them his whole life.

"Hush, now, and listen," he said, impatient. Sarah noticed none of his apprentices were in earshot. She didn't say anything more, and he kept talking. "If you truly love or care about someone, etch their name into a stone and rub a tear over it, then cast it into the deep ocean. A mermaid will give you a silver coin if your loved one is not among the waves, and a gold if they are."

"Mermaids?"

He raised a brow. "I know you were sailing for years before you took to land. Can you explain everything you've seen?" She couldn't answer, feeling those dark claws digging into her skin, dragging her deeper into the ocean, and he nodded. "Exactly. Now, listen: if you throw the coin back, the mermaid will return with more gold or treasure, and if you throw that back, they'll return again with even more. If you can throw it back thirteen times, your loved one will be returned, whole and hale. But if you take even a single piece of treasure, at any point, they'll know, and they'll take that as you've accepted their compensation. If you try to summon 'em again, they'll pull you into the water and drown you. And if you offend 'em, you'll get a corpse in return."

Sarah wasn't sure what to say. It was madness. Mermaids were just stories... weren't they? But those dark claws... there had been marks in her arms when she woke up, and she'd assumed they were from Maria gripping her as she was pulled back to the surface, though really, they'd been too far apart to be Maria's hands. "What if you get nothing at all?"

"Then your feelings weren't true, according to the legend." He rubbed the back of his neck. "I know, I know, don't say it, you think I'm a crazy old man. I'm just telling you a story I heard as a lad."

"And have you ever heard of anyone actually doing it?"

"Twice. In my great-grandfather's time, a few folks heard the story and asked him to take 'em on the water. Mostly when they threw the rock into the water he'd distract 'em and put a piece of silver on the railing, give 'em some comfort instead of saying their feelings were false. Most would assume their loved ones died in the New World. But he said there was a time or two the silver was be switched for gold, and he'd find the silver later on the shore." Tom shrugged, and it was unclear if he really believed that part.

"And the other?"

"A young woman, probably forty years past. She wasn't from here, I don't know where she called home, but she swore it was true. She went out, returned the gold and treasure thirteen times, and her sailor was returned to her, healthy and whole. They were going to try their fortunes in the New World. I saw the lad, he looked hale enough. Of course, maybe I'm wrong, maybe there's nothing out there." He shrugged. "Maybe it'll just give you some closure to give the lass a grave marker."

Sarah nodded, swallowing hard. A burial at sea may have been a sailor's dream, but it wasn't much comfort to those left behind.

"The ship repairs will take a few weeks, maybe into spring," he said, returning to business at hand. "Roger'll know where to bring her to."

"Thank you," Sarah said. "I'll let him know."

She left, her copy of the contract clutched in her hand. She remembered nights spent teaching Maria to read and write by the light of a candle while Maria taught her seafaring, helping her catch up to the rest of the crew, who had all seen her as a timid little bookworm of minimal use on a ship. But she could learn fast, and she'd proven herself capable, and she'd done it again when she gave up the sea. She gave it to Roger when she found him, back aboard the ship. As long as it stayed anchored, she wouldn't start to feel panic, though she was by no means as comfortable as she had once been.

"Alright," he said, looking it over. She and Maria had taught him to read as well. "I'll bring her 'round the next high tide."

As she walked out of the captain's quarters, she turned back to Roger. "What do you think of mermaids?"

"I'd like t'see one someday," he replied. "From a safe distance. Having served under you and Maria, I know better than to underestimate women of the sea." He gave her a sad smile.

Tom's story had created a fledgling hope in her mind, something dangerous and fragile that compelled her to act, and she couldn't bring herself to ignore it. "What if I said it might be possible?" This was crazy. She hadn't been out to sea in years. She could have happily gone far longer without ever being on a moving ship again. What was stronger, her fear of the ocean, or her love for Maria?

He frowned. "What do ye mean?"

"Well..." She told him the story. He was quiet after, but he didn't reject the idea outright.

"You want to try it, don't you?" She nodded. "We'll need to borrow a boat and go out to the open water. And you'll need to be on that boat."

She swallowed hard. "I know."

"Do you think you can do it?"

"As long as it's not stormy."

"Lass, you know that doesn't mean there won't be strong waves, and you'll feel it in a small boat." He ran a hand through his hair. "I'm not trying to discourage ye, but if yer gonna do this, there's not stoppin' halfway. Either ye do it and see it through, or ye fail and if it works or it don't, ye'll never know and ye'll never be able to try again."

"I know that." It felt like there was a weight in her stomach, but she steeled herself. "I want to do this."

"Alright, we'll meet on the docks at dawn," he said.

"Aye, Captain," she said.

His smile was sad, but she could see that he wanted this to be true as well. "Hopefully not for long."

At dawn they set out in Tom's old fishing boat. The old shipwright hadn't been surprised when she'd returned and made the request. He'd just handed her a chisel and mentioned it would work better than a knife for carving into a rock. She'd spent all night carving Maria's name into a smooth stone she'd picked up from the shore and was now in her coat pocket. Sarah had offered to help row, but Roger had taken one look at her white-knuckled grip on the edge and shook his head. He also offered to tie her to the plank that served as a seat, but she refused, as tempting as it might have been. The water was as calm as it ever was in the Atlantic Ocean, the spray freezing as it rose over the bow. She tried not to think about how it had burned going down her throat and into her lungs, how she'd spent months gasping for breath and coughing in equal measure. She shivered and pulled her coat closer around herself.

"Are ye alright?" Roger asked, pausing.

"Keep going," she said instead of answering, but he didn't move.

"Sarah."

She glared at him. "I can do this."

He watched her for a moment, then nodded and kept rowing farther out. "This should be far enough, from what Tom said."

"Okay." She pulled the stone out of her pocket, rubbing her thumb over Maria's name. "Now we just need a tear." It wasn't hard to start crying again. She wiped away a tear and smeared it over the etched letters, then paused, and almost started laughing.

"Sarah?"

"I was just thinking, I should pray that this works, but who do I pray to?" The god in the church wouldn't listen to a prayer like hers, and only fools asked favours from the sea herself.

"I have no idea," Roger said, thinking it over. "I think we might be on our own this time."

Sarah nodded and took a deep breath before reaching over the side of the boat and dropping the stone into the waves. "Now we wait." She had no idea how long it would take for something to happen, or if anything was going to happen at all. She pulled out a handkerchief and wiped her eyes. The tears wouldn't stop now that they'd started. Roger sat quietly, and she was grateful that he didn't try to tell her that it was okay, or any of the lines she'd heard people say to the women who left the dock in tears. At least it gave her something to focus on beside the motion of the ship, the spray of the cold salt water, and the terror that made her want to turn back to shore.

Sarah…" Roger's tone was odd, holding an urgency that made her look up in time to see a webbed hand covered in scales and bearing sharp claws slip back beneath the water, a gold coin left on the railing of the boat. They looked at each other with wide eyes, then back at the gold.

Sarah tentatively picked it up and dropped it back over the side, hearing it hit the water. "I want Maria back." She wouldn't be tempted by treasure. She would have given all the gold and jewels in the world to bring Maria back. Resisting it would be easy. The hand was just like the one that haunted her nightmares. It was a memory, not a dream. A mermaid had been about to collect her before Maria pulled her back.

A few minutes later, the scaled hand rose again, and this time Sara could see the top of a head of dark hair. A handful of gold coins was left this time. Sarah pushed them back over. It felt like there were iron bands around her chest, emotions she couldn't quite name running through her. This was real. This was really happening.

Tom's story had been right. Each time, more gold was left. When the first chest appeared, the mermaid rose higher out of the water to lift it over the railing, and Sarah was speechless. She was both beautiful and inhuman, with luminescent eyes and green scales in patches over her dark skin that formed gorgeous, incomprehensible patterns. The mermaid looked at them for a moment, and Sarah thought she looked curious. The end of her tail rose out of the water as she dove back down.

"By God…" Roger murmured, staring after the creature for a moment before helping Sarah lift the chest overboard without bothering to open it.

The next time, there were two of them, the next with brown hair, blue scales, and lighter skin. More treasure was handed over. Sarah made sure every single piece, down to the last tiny pearl, was returned.

"That's eight, isn't it?" Sarah said, glancing at Roger.

He nodded. "That would have bought us a whole fleet of new ships… if this is going to happen five more times… you could be as rich as any Emperor."

Sarah looked over at him. "I'm not keeping any of it." Would she have to watch him?

"I never said ye should," he said. "I can understand why others would be tempted, that's all. I want Maria back too. She's your lover, but the crew is the only family I got in the world. My family by blood, they all died with smallpox. I don't want to lose anyone else."

Sarah nodded as the next round of chests and treasure passed over the side of the boat. She had chosen to leave her blood family, so she had a different sense of loss, but she could understand his pain. "We just want Maria back," she said before the mermaids vanished beneath the waves. The first mermaid looked at her, tilting her head slightly. Sarah had no idea if they understood her words, what languages they spoke. It seemed wild that she even had to think about that. But the mermaid said nothing and vanished back beneath the waves. "Can this boat handle more treasure?" A wave of panic broke over her at the thought of the boat sinking.

"I don't think they want to sink us?" Roger said. "You're the merchant, what d'you think?"

She took a deep breath and looked, trying to remember what had been brough on board before. "There haven't been more than three chests, and the bits that are getting tossed over are getting more valuable. As long as that keeps up, I don't think there'll be a greater amount."

"Okay." He started tossing it all back, and Sarah joined in.

Despite her mental calculations, the final pile of treasure nearly did sink the boat. The edge of the railing was almost level with the water. She and Roger worked quickly to send it back to the depths. The iron bands around her chest had tightened with each piece of gold passed over the railing, each sight of the mermaids. They were so close. Sarah wasn't sure if either she or Roger took a breath as they waited. That was thirteen.

"I'm afraid to look over the edge," she admitted.

"Aye," Roger rasped in agreement. A clawed hand appeared over the side of the boat, and Sarah almost felt sick from the tension. Then a human hand appeared next to it. She and Roger almost tipped the boat as they lunged to the side to watch the mermaid help Maria rise from the water, coughing and sputtering, but very much alive.

"Maria!" Sarah pulled her over the side and held her close, uncaring that her clothes were getting soaked.

"You did it!" Maria said, cupping Sarah's face in her hands and kissing her. Sarah melted into the kiss, tears leaving warm tracks on her cold cheeks. Maria was back. She was alive, and she was there with them. The lovers only pulled apart when they had to breathe again but didn't let go of each other. "You did it. You really did it."

"Of course," Sarah replied. "You promised you'd come back. I just made sure you kept that promise."

"You're out on the water."

"I am, and I still don't like it." She looked over at Roger, who was drying his eyes.

"We'll go back," he promised, but hugged Maria tightly first. "Welcome back, Captain."

"Aye, that's right," she said as Sarah wrapped her in a blanket they'd brought along. "Bring us home."

As Roger started rowing, Sarah held Maria's hand tightly, afraid to let go of her again. She looked back at where the mermaids had been, and saw the two of them, their eyes above the water, watching. She waved cautiously and the first mermaid repeated the gesture before they both vanished beneath the sea.

"Sarah?" Maria asked.

"They were watching us," she replied.

"They are waiting for us to join them, one day," Maria said. "Not any time soon, but when we're ready, we can join them." She smiled. "If you can handle the ocean by then."

Sarah looked back once more, but only saw the waves. The mermaids were likely long gone, already far beneath the surface. "Maybe it wouldn't be so bad..."

Ash Greening

Ash Greening is an author from Eastern Newfoundland. Their fiction has appeared previously in *Kit Sora: The Artobiography* (Engen Books), *Whisper Sweet Nothings* (WANL), and *Folklore Next Door* (WANL).

Sea Change

Sweet Tommy caught a scoundrel's eye one fateful winter day,
Who swore he'd steal his heart and keep it locked away.
With eyes that shone with mischief and words so sickly sweet,
It wasn't long before the scoundrel swept him off his feet.

His scoundrel whispered in his ear a lie as old as time:
If you come to bed with me, then I'll make you mine.
So, Tommy let his scoundrel have him, time and time again.
Sheets grew cold, and lies grew old, but no ring ever came.

He was his scoundrel's secret, and he soon discovered why:
His ring was meant for someone else. His love had been a lie.
When Tommy found the happy pair in the marketplace,
His scoundrel's tongue turned vicious and left him in disgrace.

Soon Tommy's name was slandered up and down the town,
So he threw himself into the sea in hopes that he would drown.
But there was something lurking just beneath the solstice waves,
Seeking youth and beauty to grant them ocean graves.

The Siren King had come to collect his payment due,
With a smile full of shark's teeth and eyes of ocean blue.
To spare the season's ships, he had long since set his price:
At moonrise on the summer solstice, a single sacrifice.

Although the solstice sun had yet to lower in the sky,
Tommy's broken heart caught the siren's hungry eye.
He dragged him to the ocean depths but did not let him drown,
And asked for nothing in return for Tommy's ocean crown.

All that long, hot summer, the scoundrel thought him dead,
While Tommy warmed different sheets in his siren's ocean bed.
His ruined heart was filled with salt, remade by his king,
And he gained a siren's tail to replace his promised ring.

At summer's end, the scoundrel was to make his wealth at sea.
A tempest raged and moored the ship; it wasn't meant to be.
On autumn first, the scoundrel sailed off towards his slaughter,
Out where Tommy and his king were waiting in the water.

When the hull began to flood, the crew could naught but pray.
The great ship sank behind him as the scoundrel slipped away.
Six souls aboard the little boat thought they might escape;
They rowed towards the harbour shores to try and outrun fate.

How the scoundrel trembled when he beheld the sight
Of Tommy glaring down at him with all a siren's might.
The other five, they could be spared; that was Tommy's offer,
But only if the scoundrel jumped and joined him in the water.

The scoundrel didn't spare the others from a fate so grim;
He stayed aboard the boat while they were made to swim.
Four were dragged below autumn waves towards the ocean floor.
Of the five, there was only one who reached the harbour shore.

The scoundrel found himself alone with Tommy and his king.
He knew his death was coming when he heard the sirens sing.
They dragged him beneath frigid waves, down to depths unknown,
And there, the scoundrel's skull adorns sweet Tommy's ocean throne.

Jai-Lynn Francis

Jai-Lynn Francis is an avid lover of the arts from Mount Pearl, Newfoundland. Besides writing, she loves art, drawing, music, sewing, and painting. She has over forty plants and loves to research science, mythology, and the paranormal. She is also a student of language, and is currently learning French, Mandarin, and Latin.

In 2021, she won the Mount Pearl Focus on Youth Literary Arts Award, and that same year also won a flash fiction contest hosted by O'Donel High through her teacher, Melissa Bishop, who also appears in this collection.

She brings us her first published story: "Say Goodbye Before You Go."

Say Goodbye Before You Go

The puddles left behind by the most recent downpour were sent up and out when our car drove through them, but the hazy, grey mist was so thick that we could only catch a glimpse of the intense spray.

"Stay out of the potholes, Quincy." My co-worker with the dyed garnet hair held onto the grab handle above her door. Not really gripping it; a more expressive than purposeful gesture.

He ran a hand through his unruly dark blond hair, taming it just a tad. "Nancy, I've been through this. *I can't.* They're everywhere."

She giggled. "It's like he hasn't been outside of town before."

I sighed. "Yeah." Being a backseat witness to their banter made me feel like I was watching parents argue. Quin was younger than us, but nonetheless... I smiled, tired. "Watch where you're going, Quincy."

He sputtered and stammered.

The view from my window was flecked with water droplets, and beyond that I couldn't see much. I closed my eyes. Less than an hour left to go.

Short, stocky evergreens lined the highway between the sparsely located houses. The weather had cleared just enough for me to be able to see the sign when we passed it by. It was one of the few signs I got to see, along with Whitbourne, Sunnyside, Glovertown, and Gambo.

So close. I was looking forward to getting off of the highway (and out of the car). I didn't like being on it in the fog. I insinuated to the others that I wanted to drive, but Nancy was adamant about Quin driving to his first job outside of the St. John's Metro area.

We turned right off of the highway and onto a short lane before turning left onto Laurentia Cove's main road. The cracked, sun-bleached asphalt was slick with the rain that collected in the tracks made by vehicles that had driven on it before. There were fewer trees within the community. I could see homes, gardens, parked vehicles, and sheds well before we reached them. We turned left onto Fays' Road. The particular Fays we were here to see were Emily and George, the great-aunt and uncle of one of our former employees. They were amongst the scattered few people around the island who let us use their homes as a base whenever work brought us their way. A great aunt and uncle to us all.

Their little blue house was a safe haven. It brought forth memories of clear skies and boat rides, home-cooked meals and good times.

I had to wait for Quin to get out and pull his seat ahead before I could clamour out of his grey coupe. A smile came to my face as I stretched my legs, arms, and back. I could have done a lap around the Fays' yard. The weather was irrelevant. George came out to greet us, and helped Nancy with her luggage, to which she showed him gratitude. She happened to be on her summer holidays from her job as a nurse, so she decided to spend a few days out there. Emily and George always made the offer whenever we were coming to stay with them for business, so they were delighted. As was she. She was excited to go to the sandy Windmill Bight Park beach in the neighbouring community of Lumsden.

"Hello!" Emily wasted no time in giving us all hugs. She was just tall enough that the side of my head got buried in her curled, white hair when I put my arms around her. Her and Nancy gave each other a particularly tight squeeze, laughing. "How was the drive?"

With passion, we each gave her our own descriptions of the unsatisfactory weather, as Newfoundlanders do. The weather that, as Quin put it, "started when we got past Holyrood and followed us all the way here. It was wild. I could barely see the road."

He continued his theatrical tirade to Emily's amusement as George carried Nancy's suitcase by the handle up to the concrete front step. He squinted as the blustery wind blew his snowy hair into his eyes. "And it's foggier here again. Can't see a hand in front of your face down at the cove."

Nancy thanked him once more. "I bet it's freezing down there."

"Mm. It's not very nice."

Emily chuckled. "You planned a perfect day for your trip!"

The three of us, dressed in clothing we figured would

be more than appropriate for August 24th during this year of 2011, laughed, regretting some of our choices.

George got the door. He tipped his head in its direction. "Now come in before you gets wet."

His wife bubbled. "We'll have to hang 'em out on the line when the sun comes out!"

We giggled, not having to be told twice. We were offered cups of tea upon entry, and Nancy accepted. Emily and George informed us that they weren't letting us go out on our job until we ate breakfast, because they correctly assumed we hadn't eaten anything of substance yet that day.

Not that our job was very far away, as they usually were. We had been staying with the Fays for the past few years whenever we had a job in the area. It was a convenient home base when going to locations that were one, two, or three hours away.

This time, for the first time since I had been with the Society, the location was actually in Laurentia Cove, just five or so minutes away.

As I stepped around the light brown kitchen table to get to the off-white landline, Nancy was inquiring about Ryder.

George's brown eyes beamed with pride. "He's goin' to his third year in university, God love 'im."

I smiled. I dialed her number, nearly forgetting to add "1-709".

"What's he doing?" Quin drank half his glass of orange juice in one go.

George's eyes squinted in contemplation. "Science, I believe—biology!"

Emily put the salt and pepper on the table. "And he's doing something else too… ah… French."

"His minor?" Our young colleague eyed the stove with glee.

"I believe." Nancy thought he was as adorable as the rest of us did.

My girlfriend answered after a few rings. "Hi. You made it in safe?"

I giggled. In the background, I could hear the clacking of keyboards, the ringing of phones, and all the other sounds that made up the general cacophony of an office at quarter after ten in the morning.

I yawned, tracing the edges of the vertical white boards that made up the wall as I leaned against it. "The weather wasn't very nice, but we got here alright."

"Okay." She sighed, becoming transfixed by her screen for just a second. "I forgot you were going today. It was weird waking up and you not there." I could hear her furrowed eyebrows and her discontented frown. "Could you leave me a note, or text me next time? Let me know that you'll be gone."

I laughed. "I meant to. I'm sorry." I twirled the spiraled cord of the phone around my finger. "I should be coming home today though, unless something happens. My shift starts at nine."

My associates snickered about how much trouble I was in. For an instant I regarded them with a grin.

She snickered, and I could hear her scintillating brown eyes twinkle. "From things that go bump in the day to things that go bump in the night."

I chuckled. I overheard a co-worker of hers say something to her, to which she made a reply that I couldn't quite discern.

"What are you at today?"

I realized that the cord was long enough for me to be able to sit down to the right of the head of the table, so I sat. "Investigating poltergeist activity in a house down by the cove."

"Ah."

"Say hello to C for us!" Emily bubbled. George, Nancy, and Quin echoed similar requests.

"Your adoring fans say hello." We laughed together.

"Oh my…" Her voice trailed off. "Tell—" another mumble from another co-worker. "I should go."

"As should I." I twisted my fork around in my fingers. "I'll see you… this evening, or tomorrow morning."

"Tomorrow evening. You'll need sleep."

"Yeah…" The frying pans on the stove sizzled. The thick fog outside dampened the warm yellow light that emitted from the fixture on the ceiling. It felt like five in the morning hadn't passed after five hours. "I'll let you go."

"Alright. See you…"

"See you…" Gently, I laid the phone back on its cradle.

"Some sweet," chirped George, as he and Emily came around with our plates. They all laughed. I was confused.

There was no point in waiting, so at quarter to eleven after we had finished our breakfast, we got ready to go. Emily called Mike and Lorna Gulliver to tell them. We piled back into Quin's car and drove down the winding road.

The Gullivers' home had been haunted for just over five months, starting when their grandson Kyle had died in a car accident. The other car was being chased by the police. And on that icy road, the car couldn't brake fast enough to avoid him. His side of the car was hit. He was killed instantly.

It wasn't unusual for a person who died prematurely to have difficulty moving on, but it was quite unusual for a person to haunt a place they infrequently visited. Most spirits clung to the places where they died, or their homes; usually the former, likely due to frustration at their circumstances, and perhaps an inability to face the fact that they were no longer living. But the spirit of this young man had settled in his grandparents' house, a place he only stayed at each summer. And while that did explain the dramatic spike in activity that began just a few days previous, it did not explain why he was there in the first place.

Our objective was to figure that out, and upon doing so, hopefully coax him into passing on into whatever place or world was awaiting him.

George had been correct about the weather down at the cove. The Gullivers' was right next to it, separated from it by a thin barrier of trees.

I had to look at my feet to ensure that I wasn't missing the steps up to the old, dark brown house. Mike opened the door, giving us a somber "hello".

We hadn't gotten to scout the location beforehand, it being so far away, but George and Emily did. We had also spoken to Mike and Lorna several times over the previous few days, so we knew where all of the best spots were for us and our equipment, and we had all the necessary information.

I observed Nancy, as she laid a small box on the dining room table. She had the look. Calm, but deeply calculative: her eyes hardened, but not truly scrutinizing anything tangible before her.

"Is he here?"

Nancy's eyes fluttered shut as she began to respond, bringing her focus to the material world. "He... I can't confirm that it's him, but I do feel a very strong masculine energy. It's very light. It's a young man. So, not to assume, but..." She shrugged and gave me an affirmative half-smile.

I nodded. "Anything else?"

"No." She opened the box and took out a recorder, EMF reader, walkie-talkie, barometer, and thermometer. We packed lightly for this job. The Fays told us that this was their first time experiencing paranormal activity in their home, so we made the perhaps-bold assumption that there was, at most, only one spirit present. We didn't take any elaborate technology or a bigger crew. Too many people or devices in a small space would just interfere with each other; too much sound and too many energies. "I just wish he'd get close enough so I'd know what he's feeling."

Setting up only took us about fifteen minutes.

The Gullivers were friends of the Fays, and from what I understood, also relatives. Distant cousins, in-laws, or something like that. Just over a week before, one evening,

George and Emily were at their home. The subject of Kyle came up, and they reluctantly admitted that he hadn't left, that some part of him remained with them.

Emily and George told them about us, and that we could help. They were hesitant. They were concerned. To them, the whole idea felt wrong, unethically so. But they were willing to move past that to allow their grandson to truly be at rest, and for them to be at peace with that knowledge.

Their mannerisms and countenances reflected this. They greeted us with the same subdued expressions; regarded us with tired eyes and tight lips. Their movements lagged. Their voices trailed.

"Are you ready?" Nancy held Lorna's hand as the troubled woman's eyes filled with tears.

She nodded.

"Okay."

Both Emily and I had explained to the Gullivers how this process worked. They knew what they were supposed to do.

Nancy and Mike went to the living room. Quin, Lorna, and I went to the bedroom that Kyle would stay in when he visited. The bottom half of the room had cerulean wallpaper with slightly lighter vertical stripes that had a satin finish. The top half, separated from the bottom with dark brown wainscoting, was papered with white. Small pink flowers were scattered across the white in a sprawling pattern.

The bed was fitted with a blue comforter and had white cases on the pillows. Lorna sat down. Quin opted to sit cross-legged on the light floor. I stood next to the room's short, white dresser and took the room in. Across from me, on the other side of the bed, was a small window with a dark frame. I twisted the handle to open it. The symbolism was often helpful.

I moved back to my spot. The breeze from outside shifted the diaphanous blue curtains. Lorna looked at me, waiting. Our supplies were all laid out on the bed. I picked up the recorder and let my thumb rest over the red button. "Lorna, try your best to be calm if we do see or hear something, alright? We want to be inviting."

She nodded. "You may have good luck today."

I listened attentively.

"He loved bad weather. He used to like going out in it." She smiled fondly, shaking her head. "Let's go."

I hit record. "Is there anybody here with us?" I already knew a plausible answer, but just to get things started, and to hopefully draw Kyle near, I asked regardless. It was always a good way to begin. Both homeowners knew to be completely silent unless prompted to speak. Coordination was required to get a usable recording. Allowing for a pause between my queries, I continued. "Are you here with us, Kyle?"

I listened. If the poltergeist activity was of Kyle's doing, then there was a realistic likelihood that he could gather enough energy to speak at an audible volume.

"Kyle, if you're here, can you give us a sign?" I looked at Lorna, then at Quin. They both appeared to be okay. "We know you've been moving some things around… Knocking things over. Throwing things. Breaking things… Could you show us how you do that, Kyle?"

Our eyes scoured the room for any sort of indicator.

I hoped that if there was any activity elsewhere in the house, it was picked up on by Nancy and Mike. That was the benefit of having at least one tech or surveillance person on a job. Effective communication without disruptions. But this was really too small of a job and location for all of that. We'd be able to pick up on my noisy, exuberant younger brother in all of our recordings.

"Are you angry, Kyle? Are you angry that you died?" This wasn't uncommon for poltergeists. And even if it wasn't how he felt, he was likely trying to get someone's attention, so his feelings being interpreted incorrectly might rouse him to act or express himself. "How are you feeling, Kyle?" I wasn't hearing anything through my naked ear, and neither were Lorna or Quin, judging by their silence.

I had been eyeing the thermometer and barometer on and off since I had started. There were no dramatic rises or falls in temperature or air pressure. The room had the same dank chilliness as before. With all the lights in the house off, the grey, insipid quality of our surroundings was enhanced, the only illumination coming from the squall around us. All was still as I replayed our recording. Subconsciously or not, we each leaned closer, turning our heads so at least one of our ears could pick up on any faint replies.

Once or twice the device picked up Nancy's voice, but that was all we could hear.

"The recordings will get processed on our computers when we get back." Quin told the elderly woman, whose grey-white hair was frizzy with the humidity. "We can remove the background noise and we might hear something then."

"Okay." She looked a bit distraught, the creases on her eyes and forehead deepening.

I put a hand on her shoulder. "It's alright. We know he's here. We'll do our best to help him."

The walkie-talkie beeped. I picked it up. It was Nancy. "We've got him."

Quickly, but quietly, we all went single file down the short, narrow old staircase, to join Nancy and Mike at the dining room table. The Ouija board, much like the one we had upstairs, was in the centre of the surface, on top of the lacy tablecloth. Mike and Lorna sat at the heads of the table. It was easy to see that this concept perturbed them.

"Do you want to join?" asked Nancy, calmly.

The couple shook their heads, not needing any time to ponder.

We wasted no time. Nancy, Quin, and I let two fingertips of each of our hands graze the glazed wooden surface of the planchette.

The boards weren't mystical doors to another world. They were just one of many methods of channeling a spirit's energy into one we could use to further our investigation. They couldn't invite anything that wasn't already there. Or invite anything else for that matter. What we were communicating with had to already be near, to oblige.

"It's him? Did you see him?" I looked at my older co-worker. I didn't doubt her abilities, but I felt I needed to ask.

She blew a shiny strand of dyed red hair out of her eyes, her hands staying put. Her dark, steady gaze answered for her. "I didn't see him, but I feel his presence."

That answer was enough for me. "Quin." I made sure I had his full attention before proceeding. "Are you ready?"

He nodded. "I'm ready." He didn't have that child-like intrigue and wonder in his eyes when on jobs anymore. It made me proud to see him grow, especially knowing that I helped to train him. But I would praise him later. The two of us waited for Nancy to begin.

"Kyle," her voice was steady, modulated. It was low and engaging. "Do you know why you're here?"

We let ourselves gaze blankly at the board. Dissociating to take some of the pressure off the spirit that was in our midst.

It didn't take long.

The planchette moved, and in the centre of our cramped digits we could see through the circular glass Kyle's response.

C-O-V-E.

"Yes, Kyle. You're here in Laurentia Cove." She paused, giving us all space and time. Her breath was steady. She looked downward, collecting the pieces of her thoughts, knowing she could only ask one question at a time, knowing that if she lost him, she may never get him back. Also, that the spirit that was once a lively young adult was holding onto her patience and composure. Looking upward once again, she spoke just as softly as before. "What's keeping you here, Kyle?"

No hesitance.

C-O-V-E.

With all the lights off, the house was dim. The lifeless,

damp air swayed the curtains and made the room clammy and bleak. Every surface was awash with grey. The pink tablecloth, the white, floral centerpiece, the lemon-yellow wallpaper with the intricate, lacy pattern, the lustrous, glazed wooden chairs, the faces of Kyle's grandparents; they were all muted. Dull.

The three of us exchanged glances and stood. Once again, we extended an offer that we knew wouldn't be taken up.

I regarded Mike and Lorna. "Do you want to come with us?"

They shook their heads, but their once-defeated eyes now had a spark of something else beneath the numbness.

"Cut through the trees on the side of the house to get to the cove. There's a path." Mike's voice was low, but unwavering.

Lorna muttered, "He always liked it on misty days."

After descending the stairs, we went to the left side of the house. In the mist, the path wasn't difficult to find. It was wide enough for a vehicle, and it was a near-straight line. The end was a smoky grey, and not green.

The terrain underfoot was molded by years of being driven over. We walked in the flattened ruts so we wouldn't stumble trying to on the knobbly ground between them.

The air had a strong smell, I thought. The sultry air was like a soupy perfume of the scents of pine and the sea. If the smells were less natural, it would have been overbearing. Pine branches brushed off of my arm and leg as I moved. I nearly tripped on a rock. My ankle twisted enough for it to ache after Quin gripped my upper arm to help me stabilize myself.

As we came out through the widening opening of the path, it became very noticeable just how much the woods shielded us from the weather.

Droplets of moisture beat against my face in the accelerating wind, and I wasn't sure if I was warm or cold. The jeans I was wearing were sticking to my legs by the time I got clear of the trees.

I looked around. We all did. But what was there to see, even if we could? I could make out the colours of the things in the distance. The dark, descending slopes of rocks that partially enclosed Laurentia Cove, making it what it was; the blue of the rolling ocean; and the warm grey of the pebbles of the seashore. This 'beach' wasn't sandy like that of nearby Lumsden.

Strands of my light hair were plastered to my face, dripping wet. I swept them back with a hand. I squinted instinctively.

"Don't go too close!" I shouted to Quin over the wind. He regarded me over his shoulder and gave me some hand gesture before carefully moving closer to the shoreline, his form less and less distinct the further he went.

Nancy was struggling to tie back her hair with a tie she got out of her sweater pocket. The purple fabric draped off of her like leaden curtains with her arms raised. "What could be keeping him here? He may have been attached to the house, but why the Cove?" Her voice sounded more aggressive than intended with the wind and water lashing all around us.

The best theory I had was that: "It could remind him of his childhood. Help him stay in denial that he's dead."

"He knows he's dead. He's soaftlemn... It's upsetting to him, but he's accepted it."

It was all I had. "Then why would... Can you still feel him near?"

"No—I—I don't know. The weather is too distracting. He could be near, just not in our close presence." She walked closer to the shore. "If he means the water itself, maybe we'll have better luck. I'll go over there." She pointed to the left. Quin had gone to the right.

I went straight ahead. I kept my eyes to the ground. I was unable to effectively reach spirits, or know when they were reaching back, so all I could do was look for anything peculiar.

But what was there?

The wind and rain didn't mask the noise of the roaring wave that pounded the shore. Regardless of how cold it actually was, the dampness of my skin made me shudder. Ignoring that, and squinting to look through the fog as much as I could, I noticed that whatever was opposite the cove across the water was obscured from view. It looked like the water just went on forever, beyond the haze. Or, like there was nothing on the other side of the haze, like that was where the world stopped.

The air was penetrating, but I didn't let it get to me. I concentrated on the shore, the rocks, the seaweed, the scattered broken and intact shells and glass fragments. What about the geography was significant?

Could something have happened to him here? A traumatic event that his family was somehow unaware of? Or was Laurentia Cove —the cove itself —just that special to him? We could possibly get answers to these questions if we went back to the board, or maybe Nancy had already communicated with him. She didn't want to wait to act on his responses, but I knew that if he relayed to her anything useful, she would tell me.

Maybe I was looking at it too literally. I wasn't sure about Kyle's grasp of the figurative or of my own, but perhaps the infinite ocean and the opaque fog matched how he felt about the afterlife or being dead. Like it was a blind, disorienting oblivion that he would spend the rest of his existence drowning in.

Did he feel like he was between one place and another? Trying to keep his hold on the place he was from, but fighting to not be pulled into a place he didn't want to go? He was aware of his state, which maybe terrified him.

All I could do was jump to conclusions. Grasp at straws. I didn't have anything solid to go off of. What could I do? My hope was dwindling; my mind clouding over. What were we even doing out here, dooming ourselves to a case we couldn't solve?

I needed more.

"Shannon."

If I didn't know where my colleague had gone, I wouldn't have been able to distinguish where her voice was coming from. I wasted no time in going to her. I prayed she had found something of use, that she was right in thinking that going down to the water would make her better able to reach the spirit.

After some time, I saw the blurred shape of her ruby hair. Getting closer, I saw something else. I couldn't see the outline Nancy's face. She was turned nearly back on to me while she looked at something grey and moving.

"Shannon." She approached me when I was about twenty feet away, meeting me in the middle. "Come here."

Her eyes were frantic. She pulled me by the arm towards the woman in the water.

Her skin was ashen. Dark hollows were formed by her gaunt cheeks and sunken, glassy eyes. Thick visceral, pendulous tubes jutted from her head, off-white and tipped with peach, and from between them strands of dull, black hair laid flat against her forehead. Her skin was opalescent but lacked the shimmer. It was flecked with abalone, and her lips matched. Closed gill slits occupied the sides of her neck, down to her protruding collarbones. Peachy scales dotted her shoulders and chest, becoming more frequent the further down they were. Her skin was pulled tight over her ribs. She was bony and frail. Her lower half was obscured by the water, but it looked like she could have been kneeling, if she had legs or was using them.

"You're not afraid?" I asked her. Her gaze was intense and unyielding. She was not afraid.

Her exhale was a wheeze. When was the last time she had spoken? I could see her slightly pointed teeth. "The lady felt me there. She's got the sense." Her focus turned to the psychic at my side. Her eyes were sad. Filled with deep despair and longing.

We understood. And so we couldn't speak.

Nancy took a few steps into the water, slowly. She kneeled down in front of the woman and her calves and feet were submerged.

"Are you looking for Kyle?"

Nancy bowed her head as an answer.

"Is he gone?"

She met the girl's eyes. "He's gone."

The woman stared down into the watery realm of her origin, and her dark hair masked her face like curtains.

Her full body shuddered. Her salty tears joined the brine of the ocean, mixing into the unintelligibly large mass of liquid, dispersing until their addition was no longer felt.

Nancy continued, "It happened almost six months ago. It was a car accident."

I could only confirm the woman's youth when she viewed my co-worker one last time. "Thank you." She had been destroyed, but the destruction had happened long before. She was devastated, but different now. Her posture was straighter. Her arms no longer laid limp at her sides. "Thank you." She fell forward into the water, and I could see the faint glints of wet scales and hair and she swam away, even those disappearing as she went further out and downward.

I watched Nancy to ensure she got out of the water alright and waited for Quin to reunite with us. I stayed far ahead of them during our silent walk back to the house. I was shaken.

As I approached the steps, I saw the young man sat at the top of them, waiting. He was wearing a red t-shirt and blue jeans. I couldn't discern any of his facial features as he waved at me. I didn't know what to do but wave back. He faded away.

We didn't know how to best explain the situation to Mike and Lorna, but it appeared that it wasn't an explanation they were looking for. Letting them know that Kyle was at peace was all they needed.

In our haste, we hadn't formally ended the session with the Ouija board. Not that that was a problem. We hadn't summoned an entity to join us, and not a powerful, malevolent entity in particular. And nothing could be channeled simply by using the board. Nonetheless, when we returned to the dining room, the planchette was no longer over the letter E, but over the word GOODBYE.

I made sure to tell Quin how proud I was of him. It took a few hours of silent driving for me to want to, or bring myself to speak. The rest of the trip was pretty uneventful.

We had left to go back at two, so we didn't get back until after seven. Quin brought me back to the Society building to get my car, and I headed off to work. I didn't have enough time to go home before my shift began. I'd have to change into the extra set of clothes I had in my trunk —for times like these —and I'd have to order food from the bar to eat before my shift. Great.

I was sad that I didn't have time to go home. But maybe it was for the best. It gave me time to process the events of that day, without having to answer my girlfriend's many inquiries.

I found myself thinking about her as I parked my car in the nearest convenient spot to my work and started walking.

I would be going twenty-four hours without sleep. I got up at four in the morning so I could get to the Society building and we could leave for five. And I got off at three, so by the time I got home and perhaps ate, it would be after four.

But I wasn't worried about falling asleep at work somehow. I wouldn't be able to sleep until I saw her again.

Downtown St. John's at night was enjoyed by most, and not to say that I didn't think it was pretty, but I rarely took the time to take it in. After working there for a decade, I felt pretty desensitized to it all. I also didn't like being recognized by the bar regulars outside of work. Not that there was anything wrong with that demographic as a whole. Most of them were decent. Talks with them made the slower hours of my shifts go by fast. But I liked leaving my bartending at the bar, unlike my job at the Newfoundland Society for Supernatural Investigation. I had spent many long nights there on my own free will, and I had taken many case journals and notes home with me.

I speedily crossed the artificially lit street when a car in each lane stopped to allow me through. I waved slightly to each of them to give them my thanks. One of them honked a "you're welcome" back.

Sometimes C would read the files with me, head on my shoulder. Or on occasion, she would help us with research for particularly difficult cases. That was what she spent her time doing before she left for university, when she wasn't studying school subjects. Our parents had both been a part of the Society back then, and that was how we met. She was fourteen, I was fifteen. I'd listen to her ramble on about location histories, their connections to atrocities and covens; religious and other symbolism; and supernatural entity profiles. She'd inform me of vampire and werewolf pack activity, of faery sightings, and of how she got to interview a shapeshifter. She'd giggle with me as I butchered the pronunciation of whatever spell I was told to learn, to be a useful witch.

I loved both of my jobs, but my job as an investigator was one I was always excited to do.

Which was good, because sometimes opportunities arise at the most unlikely of times...

Brad Dunne

Brad Dunne is a freelance writer and editor from St. John's, Newfoundland. He began his writing career as an intern at *The Walrus* magazine and has published journalism and essays in publications such as *Maisonneuve, The Canadian Encyclopedia,* and *Herizons*. His short fiction has been featured in *In/Words, Acta Victoriana*, The *From the Rock* Series, *Terror Nova*, and, *The Cuffer Anthology*.

In October 2018, he released his first novel, *After Dark Vapours*. It was followed in September 2020 by *The Gut*. *The Merchant's Mansion* is his third novel.

He maintains a blog at braddunne.ca. He's also active on twitter (@braddunne1796) and instagram (@yoloflaherty).

Jonah's Ghosts

The water was so turbid Simon felt like he was trekking through a giant tub of molasses. A shoal of herring scattered as they approached him while his lead boots stirred some flounders hiding amongst the ocean's silty floor. The sun's light struggled to break through all the water's particulate, barely lighting the way. But Simon was used to finding his way in the dark. Using just the three tiny portals of his helmet, he finally managed to locate the wreckage of the *Clara*. He tugged his hemp lifeline twice to ask for more slack, then took a big leap aboard the sunken ship's deck.

The old frigate was now home to barnacles, urchins, and seaweed. Simon hadn't expected to find much here. This was meant to be a trial run for his new diving dress. And while he still felt the stinging cold of the Atlantic through this two hundred pound suit of canvas, copper, and rubber, it was still better than layering up several pairs of long johns only to emerge bluer than the ocean itself.

This was also a trial run for Ray who had begged him to come along. The boy was thirteen now and was ready to learn the ways of the sea. Simon hoped to teach him the craft of salvaging, something better than fishing and being beholden to the merchants. The goal was to make Ray a part of his team that he would lead on long expeditions down the Atlantic, searching for lost treasures.

But as he explored the *Clara's* bridge, Simon noticed his oxygen started to taste oily. He gave his lifeline a single hard tug to request more air.

"Damnit, Ray," he cursed aloud and gave it another tug. Nothing. He could feel the air depleting in his helmet. Panic rose in his chest. The memory of his first diving run came unbidden to his mind, a memory he fought to ignore, especially whenever he was underwater. A vivid flash invaded his mind of the crew hauling up his diving partner and removing his helmet to reveal a face twisted in painful death.

Simon took shallow breaths to calm himself without wasting too much oxygen. He reminded himself that had happened before they understood water pressure and the importance of a lifeline. Of course, what good was a lifeline if it was ignored?

He started tugging the rope repeatedly now to signal Ray to haul him up. When he didn't feel the cable dragging him upwards, fresh new panic swelled. Now, instead of the image of his dead diving partner, he saw the stacks of corpses lining the field of Beaumont-Hamel. Rifle fire and mortar shells popped and burst in his ears. He was so overwhelmed that he didn't realize the cable was dragging him towards the surface. Bursting through the water, he saw Ray standing aboard the *Leigh*, manning the cable's crank. Simon grabbed hold of his boat's ladder and pulled himself up. He fidgeted frantically at the bolts on his breastplate to loosen his helmet, but his gloves were too cumbersome. Ray helped and together they managed to pull the copper and brass bell off Simon's shoulders. Before he could get to the boots, Simon pushed him away and held up his hand.

The sounds of war grew fainter with each breath Simon drew. Quick shallow gasps transformed into deep, plentiful inhalations followed by slow, restorative exhalations. The key, Simon had discovered, was not to fight it. When the memories came, he just had to ride them out. Relax the body and the mind eventually came along. The smell of salt water and the sound of seagulls replaced the iron taste of blood and the percussive assault of gunfire. He looked around and saw that he was off the coast of Newfoundland and not in Northern France. A warm sun dappled the ocean's gentle waves — an uncharacteristically beautiful summer day in Placentia Bay. The Great War was over. They were just memories and they couldn't hurt him.

He turned to look at Ray who stood sullenly with his eyes on his feet.

"You have to mind the lifeline," he said. "Don't you understand that when I tug it means I need air? That I need air to breathe?"

The boy remained silent.

"Hey," Simon said. "Look at me. Explain yourself."

"There were some whales breaching over there." Ray pointed towards the horizon where gulls circled in the sky.

Simon looked into Ray's greyish blue eyes, the colour of gun metal. He searched for some semblance of himself in the boy, but it wasn't there. He looked just like his mother, except for the eyes. Ray looked away self-consciously, turning his attention back to his feet.

"Not a great first day," Simon said. "If I'm going to set out on my own and take longer trips down to Carolina, I'm going to need a reliable crew. I was really hoping you'd show me you were mature enough for this responsibility."

Ray struggled not to cry. Simon realized he'd probably taken it too far. He wanted to reach out and ruffle the boy's hair, tell him it okay, that they'd try again soon. But he was still wearing the suit.

"Here," he said. "Help me out of this."

After Simon got out of his diving dress, they made a silent trip home, arriving late. Other men and their crews, their sons among them, were stowing their gear away in their sheds. They saw Simon and gave him friendly nods, but he knew what they said about him in private. Giving up fishing to salvage full-time was the sort of thing you just didn't do in a place like Corbin Head. At first, most people thought it was innocent enough. Maybe a bit of eccentricity following his time in the Great War. At least he wasn't cooped up in his house all day like Gerry Fagan. But then he started having success, finding valuable stuff amidst the wreckage. In a couple weeks, he could make what he'd earn a whole year at the fish. He was getting job offers from St. John's to join salvaging trips all across the coasts of Newfoundland. Some were curious and happy for him. He often had a captive audience at the pub over a few jars telling stories of his underwater escapades. Many, though, were resentful. Some of it was jealousy. Simon had found a way out of the fishery where most were chained for the lives. He owned his own boat and all his gear and owed nothing to the merchant. For others, though, it was like grave robbing. *Disturbing Jonah's Ghosts*. Simon didn't see it like that. All that treasure seemed like a waste to be left underwater.

Simon and Ray finished putting the gear away then took the dirt road home. The evening sky was painted shades of orange and red with pink cotton-candy clouds. Dusk's soft amber light polished the couple dozen biscuit and saltbox houses of Corbin Head. A blur of movement in Simon's eye caught his attention. He looked up and saw Gerry Fagan's window was open, but no sign of Gerry himself.

When Simon entered his home, he was immediately swarmed by his two daughters. He got down and hugged them both, looking into their brown eyes. Three children was a small family by outport standards, but the two girls were enough to quell any rumours.

"We already ate, Daddy," they explained. "Mommy said you were too slow."

"That's alright," he said. "Me and Ray will have a late supper."

Molly took up two plates of salt fish, potatoes, and Swiss chard with mustard pickles for Simon and Ray. After consuming his super in swift silence, Ray left the table and went to bed without dessert. Once Molly got the girls into bed, she came down and sat with Simon, who was having a mug of tea with some buttered raisin buns.

"Hannah Fagan was over earlier," she said.

"Oh?" Simon answered.

"Wanted to know if you were going to visit Gerry."

Simon sipped his tea and didn't answer.

"It's been thirteen years," Molly added.

Again, Simon was silent.

"How was Ray today?" she asked after a sigh.

"Didn't go as well as I'd planned."

"He was very quiet at supper. I hope you weren't too hard on him."

"Boy needs a stern hand if he's going to be out in boat. My father was no different."

"Did you find anything valuable today?"

"No. But that wasn't the point. It was meant to train the boy."

"It's just that it's been a while since you did."

Simon gripped his mug tightly, ready for an argument.

"Might be time you gave it up," Molly suggested.

"I'm just about ready to make my own excursions. I won't have to depend on contracts from Smith MacKay in St. John's and can keep all the profits for myself."

"Go down the graveyard of the Atlantic in Carolina?"

"That's right." Simon didn't like Molly's dismissive tone.

"And what about after that? Will that be enough to retire?"

"How am I supposed to know that?"

"I want you to think realistically about our prospects. Ray needs to learn how to fish. Salvaging isn't a viable trade."

Simon chewed his cheek. He knew she was right, but a smouldering sense of resentment towards her wouldn't let him give in. "I suppose you want me back in Percy Phippard's pocket? Maybe you want to go back to being his maid?"

That name, rarely spoken in the house, had a way of igniting the acrimonies that lay smouldering under the surface of their relationship. He watched Molly's brown eyes go black with anger.

"Won't you listen to sense?" she demanded. "Why do you spite me so?"

Simon looked away. He could feel his patience giving way to his temper. The episode underwater today had exhausted all his self-control and he was craving confrontation. "You know the reason. I'm no fool. I can subtract nine months from the time I came home."

Molly refused to acknowledge the tears streaming down her cheeks. "You don't understand, when Phippard found out his son died and that you and Gerry were coming home..."

"You decided to equal the balance?"

"It's not like I had a choice in the matter!" she hissed.

Before Simon could respond, they heard the creak of wood. They paused and looked towards the staircase. Tiny footsteps scurried back up to the second floor. After exchanging knowing glances with Molly, Simon got up from the table and went upstairs. He peeked in through Ray's door. The boy lay in his bed, pretending to be asleep, but Simon could see his blankets rise and fall with his rapid breath. He felt like he should go in and try to explain to him that none of this was his fault, ruffle his hair, comfort him; he wasn't wearing the diving dress. Instead, he closed the door silently and went to his own bed.

The next morning, shortly after dawn, Simon and Ray were at the wharf, getting ready for another expedition. The harbour was alive with the activity of fishermen getting ready for a day out on the water. It had the makings of a large day, fulfilling last evening's red sky. The ocean rested like a still mirror beneath the warm summer sun. As Simon looked out over the horizon, he thought about giving up these salvaging expeditions and returning to the fish. If he held out much longer, he'd squander the nest egg he'd built for himself and would be back to where he'd started. Yes, there was a chance he could find untold treasures down in Carolina, but most likely it wouldn't be enough to retire and live a life of leisure. Worse, it could be a fool's errand, and he'd end up in the hole worse than he'd ever be if he'd just stuck to fishing. Maybe Molly was right, maybe it was an inevitability. The question was whether he could swallow his pride and go back to working for Percy Phippard.

As he mulled these thoughts over, a small, unfamiliar boat appeared at the harbour's narrows. Others began to notice and a crowd formed. As the boat pulled near, Simon could see it carried an old man with a young blonde girl and large chest in between them. The man rowed the small lifeboat while the girl huddled beneath a woollen blanket.

"Ahoy!" the man cried out. He pulled up to a wharf and a few fishermen came to help them out of their boat.

"We've been in a terrible accident," the man explained in a British accent. "My name is Janus De Vries. My wife and I were on a ship bound for New York when we ran aground a few miles southwest of here. The ship sunk and, sadly, we were the only survivors."

The men looked back and forth between the old man with his pockmarked face to his beautiful, young bride with more than a bit of jealousy.

"How are you doing, my dear?" someone asked her. "Do you need some new clothes? I'm sure my wife could help you."

"I'm afraid she doesn't speak much English," the man explained. "She's Dutch."

The fishermen nodded and grunted.

"As you can understand," De Vries said, "we've had a very trying night. If someone could provide us with accommodations until the next coastal boat arrives to take us to St. John's, we shall be very much obliged."

Ned Rose volunteered his hospitality. De Vries thanked them while the girl remained silent, fidgeting with her wedding ring. Simon noticed that she kept that hand clenched, like it might slide right off her finger if she weren't careful.

"Oh, I hope I'm not overextending your charity if ask you to help me carry our belongings. This should be enough."

De Vries produced two gold coins and held them out for Ned. The fishermen, unaccustomed to seeing cash, let alone in this amount so casually offered, stared even more covetously than they had for De Vries' wife.

"Oh, uh…I can't, sir," Ned stammered with eyes fixed

on the money.

"Please, I insist." De Vries took Ned's hand and shoved the money into his palm. Ned rolled them around, unsure if they were real.

Junior Pennell came then and offered Ned help with the chest.

"Good man," De Vries applauded and gave a copper to Junior.

Ned and Junior stepped into the small lifeboat to haul up a large chest. They both struggled with the weight.

"Follow me," Ned said to the couple, before he and Junior began to lug the chest towards his house.

"G'day, gentlemen," De Vries announced to the crowd of fishermen, trailing after Ned and Junior with his young, silent wife.

Simon recognized the same smug expression in the De Vries' face as Phippard's. That look that said, *I have money, more money than you peasants could understand, so I own you, I own the ground you walk on*. Except De Vries didn't wear it so subtly, like a new pair of shoes that weren't moulded to your feet yet.

His story didn't add up either. The ship had sunk off a few miles southwest? Last night had been as clear and calm as anyone could ask of the North Atlantic. No skipper worth his salt would crash under those conditions. And that chest? The boat was sinking, and they were the only survivors, but they'd managed to load all their possessions aboard a lifeboat?

Simon ran to catch up with the procession. "Excuse me, sir," he said to De Vries.

"Yes, my man."

"Could you tell me the name of your ship?"

"The *Commerskie*. What for?"

"I'll wire the details to St. John's, and they can send the information back to England or New York. I'm sure the families of the deceased would want to hear as soon as possible what happened."

"Of course," De Vries muttered. The sudden dint in that smug expression was nice. Simon figured the man didn't expect such a miniscule outport to have wireless — and certainly not a scuba diver. But Simon was going to keep that last bit to himself, for now.

"Would you mind telling me what happened?" Simon asked.

"As I said, we ran aground."

A new crowd began to form to watch this terse exchange. Simon could feel some of the locals glaring at him, as if to say, *Don't look a gift horse in the mouth*.

"I'm just a little confused," Simon explained, "because the last couple of days, we've seen such clear weather."

"The warm and cool air met to form some unexpected fog and I couldn't see—"

"Oh, you were the skipper?"

There were some audible gasps at this revelation. A captain who abandoned his ship in distress? That could be criminal.

"No, no," De Vries stammered. "I merely meant to say that I couldn't see, so likely the captain couldn't either."

The onlookers nodded at this, but Simon could see they weren't convinced, and neither was he. But he was going to leave it at that.

"Do you know the general location of where she

sank?" Simon asked.

"Oh, maybe a couple miles southwest of here. We've really been through quite the ordeal, and I'm unfamiliar with this area."

"Of course, thanks. Sorry for bothering you. Just wanted to get the details clear. By the way, you speak English very well for a Dutchman."

"I was schooled in England," De Vries grunted then turned away.

The procession to Ned Rose's house resumed. Simon turned back towards the harbour. He approached Brian Meehan.

"I'm going out to check that location De Vries gave me," Simon explained. "I could use you and your crew's help."

"I don't want any trouble," Meehan replied.

"Come on, Brian," Simon countered. "You can't tell me you believe his story? He's practically laughing at us, throwing his money around, trying to buy our silence. The coaster will be here any day. We've got to do it before it arrives."

Meehan was silent, but Simon could see he was getting through to him.

"The least we can do is give those poor souls a burial," Simon said.

"Alright," Meehan responded. "Get your gear ready. I'm only spending one day at this."

Simon sprinted to his stage and started hauling out his gear. Ray followed and helped. Meehan and his crew got into the *Leigh*. Ray was about to step onto the deck when Simon seized his arm.

"You can't come on this trip," he said.

"Why?" Ray asked.

"There's going to be dead bodies," Simon explained. "A lot of them. And they're not going to look like they're sleeping, do you understand? They're going to be bloated and nasty. I don't want you to see that."

"I can handle it!"

"You're brave for thinking that. But the truth is that no one can handle it. It'll haunt you for the rest of your life."

Ray looked at Simon with tears in his eyes. Simon flinched at his gaze, unable to meet those watery, gunmetal eyes.

"C'mon, Raymond," Simon said. "Be a big boy."

Ray muttered something.

"What did you say?" Simon asked.

"Why do you hate me?"

Simon felt an immediate bubble of rage rise from his chest and was about to admonish the boy for stepping out of line, embarrassing him like this on the wharf in front of the other men. But he soon felt ashamed by this reaction. Somehow his thoughts had betrayed him and leaked into his tongue, always present behind his words, and the boy had absorbed them. He wanted to explain to Ray that he didn't hate him, that he loved him, but, well, it was all very complicated, and Simon had never been very good with words. What he realized too late was that he ought to just hug the boy, that would've been good enough, but Ray silently turned and began trudging towards home. Simon turned back to the *Leigh*. Meehan and his crew pretended not to have witnessed that exchange.

Knowing Placentia Bay and its coasts well, Simon suspected where the *Commerskie* likely ran aground. There was a small, isolated cove a few miles southwest of Corbin Head called *L'Anse aux Diable*. The devil's bay. Simon had to grin to himself.

As they approached the centre of the bay, the crew began to murmur to each other about something: bodies. Where were all the corpses? They should be floating in the water or washed ashore, but they were conspicuously absent.

"Do you suppose De Vries lied?" Meehan asked.

"Only one way to find out," Simon replied.

With the suit laid out on the deck, Simon got down and started the tedious process of getting dressed. First, he climbed feet first into the neck of the canvas dress, which was impossible to perform gracefully, no matter how many times he did it. After that, he sat down and the crew helped him with his lead boots. Last came the helmet. Simon couldn't shake feeling that he was being sealed into his casket during this part. The boys lowered the metal veil over his head and twisted it home. They tightened the series of bolts on the breastplate that connected it to the dress. Simon's sensory world was now reduced to three tiny portals and the smell of copper. He walked around to get reacquainted with the suit's bulk. Once they connected the umbilical cord from his helmet to the air pump on deck, tied his hemp lifeline to his suit, and attached him to the thick heavy cable, he was ready to be lowered into the water. Simon felt the bitter embrace of the Atlantic just as his shins dipped below the surface. Once his head was under, he took short breaths to get used to the oily air filling his helmet. He drifted slowly downwards to the ocean floor like a dream with a bag of tools in his hand.

It didn't take him long to locate the *Commerskie*; it was a pretty big passenger ship. Not the *Titanic* by any means, but certainly enough for about fifty passengers and crew. She lay diagonally on her side, strips of canvas fluttering from her rigging likes clothes on a line. Simon clamoured up onto the deck, struggling to keep his balance.

That's when he saw her, hair swaying to the waves' rhythm like seaweed — a woman tied the main mast. Her head was tilted away from Simon, almost coy and flirtatious. Dread swelled in Simon's chest, but he was able to keep himself together. From his bag of tools, he retrieved a saw and cut the poor woman loose, sending her up to the surface.

Searching the deck for more signs of death, his trepidation grew. The only murder he'd ever experienced was on the battlefield, and that wasn't technically murder, was it? No, he wasn't going to think about that right now. As he approached the cabin, he saw his second horror of the day: the doors had been boarded shut. How? Why? The answers to these questions were obvious enough, but Simon struggled to comprehend the will needed to perform such an act. There was a crowbar in his bag, and he knew that he was going to have to pry that door open to see what he suspected was behind it, but he couldn't do it. Instead, he stood there, still, unable to move. He tugged on his lifeline once to request more air. Closing his eyes, he fought to focus his mind, push away the anxiety. After a few deep breaths, he pulled out his crowbar and got to work.

Just as the boards were pulled away, the doors burst open and half a dozen corpses floated towards him, swarming him. Simon screamed inside his mask and fell backwards, struggling to get away from the ghouls. In an instant, he was back in Beaumont-Hamel, his own scream transformed into the screams of his fellow soldiers. The gunfire and mortar rounds were too loud; his eardrums were about to pop. Before him was a bloody field of young men, boys really, dead and stacked atop each other, and he wandered amongst them in this ridiculous diving suit. He struggled to keep his balance. Looking down, he saw that he was treading across a lumpy mound of khaki, mud, and flesh. He needed to get the helmet off. If only he could get it off and breathe some fresh air.

As he fumbled with the bolts with his thick gloves, he realized where he was. He was down in the Atlantic, off the coast of Newfoundland, not Northern France. It was okay, he was safe, nothing could hurt him in this suit. By repeating this to himself over and over like a mantra, his perception gradually latched onto reality. He focused on his cold surroundings, the oily texture of the air he breathed, and the metallic smell of his helmet's copper — and visions of the Great War faded. He looked up and saw the *Commerskie's* passengers floating towards the surface. But he couldn't leave yet. The cabin's entrance was yawning open before him like a tomb. He had to go down and see.

It was a nightmare. Simon surmised that the several bodies he'd encountered at the cabin's entrance had spent their final moments trying to beat the door down to get out. Most of the passengers, however, seemed to have accepted their fates and stayed in their quarters, perhaps trying desperately to make peace with God in the last moments they had. There had to be about fifty lost souls down here, he guessed. It would take several boats to get them all out. Something bumped into his leg. It was the body of a small child drifting through the water.

Unable to witness anymore, he got back up to the deck and tugged on his rope three times. The pull of the cable was a relief. As he was drawn to the surface and the wreck of the *Commerskie* shrank away from him, he felt his chest loosen.

Just as the men helped Simon get his mask off, he said: "We have to get back to Corbin Head. Now!"

Meehan set a course home and Simon explained to the men what he'd found. The corpses he'd floated to the surface lay on the deck, covered with tarpaulin. Simon could see the long slender arm of a woman poking out. Her ring finger had been severed.

Simon swung open Ned Rose's door and found Janus De Vries sitting to the dinner table with his young wife, dotted on by the Roses.

"You murdered them!" Simon shouted, his finger pointing at De Vries.

"I've no idea what you're talking about," De Vries replied, clinging to that smug tone.

"You boarded up the cabin and sunk the ship."

De Vries and his wife both looked at each other and

turned fish grey.

"H-h-h-how?" De Vries stammered.

"Bet you didn't expect to find a scuba diver in outport Newfoundland?"

De Vries broke down and explained everything. His name was really Andrew Daily, and he was indeed the captain of the *Commerskie*. He'd set sail from England, carrying six hundred tons of iron and over fifty Dutch immigrants — and his wife. But the young lady wasn't his wife. She was engaged to the real Janus De Vries as part of an arranged marriage and was miserable. They were supposed to get married in America. At some point during the long voyage across the Atlantic, she'd managed to seduce Daily and convinced him of the plan. First, Daily persuaded all the passengers to entrust him with their valuables and money into the locked chest to avoid the possibility of theft. Familiar with Newfoundland's coast, Daily picked *L'Anse aux Diable* because he knew he could row to Corbin Head easily enough. Then, he boarded up the cabin and ran the ship aground, knowing that it would sink quickly given its heavy cargo.

"*Idioot!*" the girl shrieked with a thick Dutch accent and started slapping wildly at Daily's head. The ring flew from her finger onto the floor and rolled towards Simon who picked it up.

He laughed to himself. "T'was you who gave it away."

The girl stopped her assault and glared at him.

"Yes, the trunk was suspicious," Simon continued. "Seemed strange that the only survivors of a shipwreck would lug that thing into a lifeboat. But people can be selfish. No, what really started the gears turning in my mind was this ring. It fit so poorly on your finger — it just couldn't be yours. That's when I knew I had to go looking."

The girl collapsed into her chair weeping, and Simon could see clearly how she had meant for this all to play out. She was going to abandon this poor fool with whatever gold she could swipe from the chest just as soon as they reached New York, where she'd find some other poor fool. Starring at the floor in disbelief, perhaps Daily was realizing this now too. Perhaps he was realizing now that he'd been tricked into committing mass murder, thinking he was going to be rewarded with a pretty young bride and a life of luxurious leisure.

Simon walked towards the door, then paused. "Who was the woman tied to the mast?"

"My wife," Daily mumbled. "She discovered what we were doing at the last minute."

"I thought so. The coastal boat will take you to St. John's where the RNC will decide what to do with you."

"They can't stay here!" Ned Rose protested. "I'll not have murderers in my house!"

"I'll keep them in the shed on my stage," Meehan offered. "We'll need to set up some kind of guard duty."

"Yes," Simon agreed. "If only to protect them from some of the people here dragging them out and throwing them in the harbour."

"They'll hang us," Daily blubbered to himself. "They'll hang us for this."

Simon felt uncomfortable in his Sunday best, wandering around Percival Phippard's house. The merchant was throwing a party in Simon's honour, as well as Meehan and his crew. Daily and his accomplice had been taken to St. John's and into the hands of the RNC. Word was they were going to be extradited to London where Daily would be hanged and the girl sent to a women's prison for the rest of her life. It had taken several longliners to carry the remaining bodies of the *Commerskie*. They were buried in a mass grave beside the Corbin Head cemetery.

Everyone else at the party seemed as uncomfortable as Simon. Most of them had never stepped foot in Phippard's house and seemed afraid to break anything. No one was even sure if they were supposed to be celebrating given the circumstances. Mostly, though, Simon didn't like being in the crowded house; it made him feel claustrophobic. He managed to find a small, unoccupied living room where he could finally breathe.

The room's walls were crowded with photographs. Many of them were of Phippard's son, James. Simon, James, and Gerry Fagan had travelled together to St. John's before heading over to Europe. In one photo, James stood in his uniform with a stoic expression on his face. A brave young soldier, ready to do his duty for God and country, no questions asked. He was a nice enough young man from what Simon could remember. Certainly didn't deserve to die. But how many thousands of young men could that be said of who'd died in the Great War?

The background babel of conversations morphed into

rifles popping. Soldiers shouted. Simon heard the piercing whistle of an incoming artillery shell. He felt himself being pulled away to Beaumont-Hamel.

"Do you have a uniform like that?"

The question whipped Simon back to the here and now. He shuddered and looked down to find Ray startled by his reaction.

"Uh, yes," Simon stammered. "Locked away in the attic."

"Can I see it?"

"Maybe. Someday."

Ray looked disappointed. Simon couldn't explain that he didn't want to see that uniform ever again in his life if he could manage it. Something else he'd have to keep from the boy. Thankfully, he'd fought in the war to end all wars and Ray would never have to worry about experiencing what he did.

Percy Phippard entered the room with his nose held up like he couldn't stand the smell of these peasants in his house. He could see they were looking at the picture of James.

"I want to thank you for your service to Corbin Head," Phippard said to Simon and held out his hand.

Simon considered breaking the merchant's jaw, but instead took his hand with a firm shake, swallowing the soft flesh of Phippard's palm within his calloused paw. Phippard winced for just an instant, but it was enough to make Simon's night.

"Is this young Raymond?" Phippard asked, turning his covetous eyes to the boy. He'd regained that smug sense of ownership.

"Yes," Simon said, putting an arm on the boy's shoulder. "This is my son."

The merchant considered Simon with his gunmetal eyes. Simon returned his gaze.

"You have a beautiful family," the merchant said and turned away. He stood in the doorway with his arm outstretched, silently ushering Simon and Ray out of his family shrine.

Molly found them with the two girls. "I think we should leave—"

"Molly," Phippard said, his eyes gleaming. "The house hasn't been the same without you."

Molly looked down at the floor, unable to speak. Ray and the girls looked at her, confused. The urge to break this man's jar once again occupied Simon. He reached his arm around Molly's waist and drew her close.

"I'm sure you'd love to have her back," he said, "but she's got her hands full with us."

Phippard flashed a terse grin then turned away. Molly smiled at Simon and they left.

The night's crisp air was a relief for Simon after spending all that time in the merchant's stuffy house. Unobstructed, the stars shone brilliantly in the cloudless sky. On the walk home, something caught Simon's attention from the periphery of his vision. It was Gerry Fagan's bedroom window. It was open and Simon could see the flickering light of a candle.

"You go on ahead," Simon said to Molly who nodded and resumed walking with the rest of the kids. Ray looked back and smiled at his father.

Simon knocked on the Fagans' door and Hannah answered.

"How lucky are we to enjoy a personal visit from the local hero," she said.

Simon didn't respond. Hannah quietly stepped aside for him to enter. He went up the stairs to find Gerry sitting a rocking chair. A soft amber glow from the solitary candle lit the room enough for Simon to see how his friend had aged. Gerry was gaunt not just in body but in soul too. Gerry looked at Simon with the same haunted stare he'd had when they left Europe thirteen years ago.

"Hello, Ger," Simon said.

Gerry gestured towards a small chair opposite him. Simon sat.

"Hannah told me all about the *Commerskie*," Gerry said. His voice was low and metallic, like his vocal cords had gone to rust from lack of use. He seemed to struggle to get even those few words out.

Simon nodded, unsure what to say.

Gerry sighed. "I understand why you haven't visited me. Everyone thinks I've gone cracked."

"That's not why," Simon said.

"Then what is it?"

"I don't want to think about it. The war. The things we saw. None of it."

Gerry nodded. They were silent for awhile then.

"How do you do it?" Gerry asked. "I can't stop. The bodies — I see them whenever I close my eyes. I can't sleep at night because it feels like I'm back there, in the trenches. Then, when I dream, there's rats everywhere—"

"Some things have to stay buried," Simon said, "so you can go on living."

"But how?" Gerry demanded. "How, dammit! I don't want to be thinking about it, but I have no control over it."

"I can't control it either," Simon admitted. "It's like a storm that comes and surprises you. It can be a beautiful clear day and out of nowhere, thunderclouds form and you're caught in the middle of it. And sometimes it feels so real, like I'm right back there."

"Yes! Exactly!"

"But this storm can't hurt you. Build a suit of armour around your mind and wait it out. Eventually they'll get weaker, the memories. They won't go away — at least they haven't for me, yet — but they'll get more manageable."

"I'm not sure I can do that."

"Yes, you can."

"I'm too weak. Those bastards chewed us up and spat out nothing but bones."

"Maybe. But you're still strong if you believe it."

Gerry looked at Simon with those haunted eyes then stared out the window. Simon stood up and left Gerry to mull it over. He walked home and quietly went upstairs. Before joining his wife, he stepped into Ray's room. A sliver of moonlight illuminated his hair, copper like Molly's. Simon crouched down and kissed his son on the cheek then joined his wife. He undressed and got into bed. They made love for the first time since conceiving their youngest daughter. After, with his defences disarmed, Simon cried into her back, nearly shaking the bed with his heaving sobs. Molly held his hand tightly, keeping him steady, glued to the here and now.

Peter J Foote

Peter J. Foote is a bestselling speculative fiction writer from Nova Scotia, Canada. He runs the FictionFirst Used Books, specializing in fantasy and sci-fi titles. He also cosplays with his wife, and alternates between red wine and coffee as the mood demands.

Many of Peter's stories are a reflection of his personal life, as he is a firm believer in the adage that a writer should write what they know.

Peter's work has twice been awarded the Kit Sora Flash Fiction Prize: once in March 2018 and again in September 2018. Peter holds the distinction of being one of only a handful of authors to be featured in all the modern *From the Rock* collections to date.

In total, Peter has been featured in over two dozen publications, with interest in his short fiction worldwide.

As the founder of the group "Genre Writers of Atlantic Canada," Peter believes that the writing community is stronger when it works together.

In 2021, he released his first novella *Boulders Over the Bermuda Triangle* through Engen Books.

Waves Remember

Feelers of the cold reached out and parted the warm waters near the shore. Few realized they were the vanguard of a monster. Caplin swam for calmer waters, crabs scurried for protection under heavy rocks, and tiny pebbles shifted and clattered: drums heralding a coming battle.

"How much longer can you keep this up, Gil?" Percy said as he tossed the burlap bag of dried beans to the lighthouse keeper, rocking with the motion of his boat, a skill second nature to one who lived on the water.

"Long enough, and then a bit longer, now hand over that box of salt cod and come inside; we have time before the storm hits," Gil said to his friend as he dropped the beans onto the dock and reached out a calloused hand. "Tea's steeped and I still have some raisin cake. You can lecture me when we're both warm."

Percy looked at the clear blue sky, and then at his friend's retreating back. "Storm?"

A wave of warmth pushed against the two men as they hurried into the keeper's house. The wooden door swung closed on well-oiled hinges, as if it wanted to keep the heat within the timber building.

As the two men pulled their damp oilskin coats off and hung them on the appropriate wooden pegs in the mud, the tabby cat curled into a wicker basket by the coal stove took note. While it didn't open an eye, its tail flicked twice and one ear tracked the men as if it were a rifle sight as they laid their bundles upon the table. A pink nose twitched as it smelled the cod, but not hearing the box open, surrendered itself to the warmth of the fire.

"I see Boots is as friendly as ever," Percy said as he helped his long-time friend put away his monthly groceries.

"We have an understanding. I don't tell him how to catch rats, he doesn't tell me how to polish the lens, and we split the salt cod. It suits us. Now make yourself comfortable and I'll see to tea," Gil replied and waved his friend towards the kitchen table.

From long experience, Percy ignored the chair draped in the knitted crimson shawl at the table, and dragged the stool that lived under the spiral staircase to the kitchen table.

"You don't need to do that, Ada won't mind it if you sat in her chair," Gil called out from the pantry.

Replaying the same conversation the pair had every month, Percy replied, "Stool is just better for my back." The lie was comfortable for both men. Listening to his lifelong friend putter away in the pantry, Percy looked out the window at the coal shed and the flagpole on the grassy hillside. The red and white sock at the top of the flagpole hung limp. "What coming storm?" Percy muttered as he turned away from the window and looked around Gil's house.

The kitchen was plain, common for 1940s Newfoundland. A narrow counter housed an enameled sink, a wooden dish rack stacked with clean dishes, and a galvanized hand pump that Percy knew drew from the cistern below them. Likewise, the rest of the kitchen, and in fact the home, was plain and spartan. The only bits of colour were the curtain Percy's wife made two years ago and Gil's Sea Gallantry Medal.

Leaning across the table, Percy fingered the heavy medal where it sat pinned to the wall above the table before looking at the faded newspaper clipping. Held together with tape, Percy read the seventeen-year-old clipping.

Tragedy strikes Southern Newfoundland.

In the late evening of August 17th, 1916, the outport ferry Burgeo captained by Calvin Turnbull was caught up in an unseasonable storm, driven off course and ran aground on the Boar's Head rocks within sight of the nearby lighthouse.

Luckily, lighthouse keeper Gilbert Faulkner was on duty and rowed his dory out to the stricken craft. Finding the captain unconscious, Faulkner sprang into action and made three trips to the stricken ferry and saved fourteen souls, but sadly not his wife.

Unknown to Faulkner, his wife Ada was returning early from visiting her ill mother in St. John's and in the confusion, and with the captain out of his wits, no one remembered she was onboard. Her remains have not been recovered.

For his bravery and courage, Governor Fahey awarded Gilbert Faulkner the Sea Gallantry Medal at a private ceremony at Government House.

Hearing his friend come up behind him, Percy leaned away from the medal but knew Gil had seen him. "You deserve that," Percy said as he waved at the medal. "No matter what you think."

"It's just a tool," Gil said and thumped the tray down with more force than necessary. The lid of the teapot rattled as if scared. "My coal shovel is more useful, but it's kept me here."

Percy swallowed and lowered his eyes, unsure of how to break the news to his friend. As Gil poured the tea, Percy reached inside his knitted vest and pulled out a small packet of mail and laid it upon the table as if the paper would shatter.

Gil paused the pouring of the tea for a moment as his eyes took in the mail stamp of "Government House, Dominion of Newfoundland" but said nothing, and returned to the tea. Passing his friend a cup, Gil pried open a metal tin, and unfolded the contents from its waxed paper wrapping. As Gil sliced the raisin cake, he spoke. "It might be a little dry, but it's good for dunking," and placed four slices upon the overturned lid of the cake tin. "Help yourself."

As the two men sat, drank tea, and nibbled on the cake, Boots stood up in his basket, stretched, and padded over to Gil where he tapped the man's leg with a paw. "It's cake. You don't like cake, remember?" The paw patted the leg again. "Fine," Gil said and broke off a thumbnail sized piece of the raisin cake and dropped it in front of the tabby. When he looked back up, he saw Percy's eyes glued to the letter between them, and tea dripping from a piece of cake in his hand.

"Fine," Gil said as he rolled up the remaining cake. "You read it if you're so curious," and pushed the mail towards the other man. "Though I suppose we both know what's inside."

"Dear Mr. Faulkner," Percy began.

"Forget all that, Percy, get to the meat of it," Gil said as he picked up the uneaten piece of raisin cake from the floor and tossed it into his empty teacup.

Percy scanned the letter, twisting it so the afternoon light highlighted the typed page. The watermark of the expensive paper cast a stencil upon the plain kitchen table.

"...as has been conveyed on many occasions, the government is replacing most of its lighthouses with automated stations, thereby freeing up needed resources and skilled labour. Considering your dedication to duty, along with being a recipient of the Sea Gallantry Medal, the government will award you a yearly pension of $800.00 for your long service once you have laid down your long-tended responsibilities."

Gil held up his hand, stopping his friend.

"But, Gil, there's more."

"I heard the important bit. I leave and they pay me off. What do they think I am, a politician?"

"It's a generous deal, Gil, think about it. There's a cottage three doors down from us you could get. Old Mrs.

Porter is going to move in with her daughter in St. John's. We could see each other daily instead of once a month."

"No," Gil said and stood. Percy watched as his friend gathered up the remains of their tea and took the tray to the counter. With his back to his friend, Gil spoke. "I can't leave her again. I did all those years ago and I won't do it to her now. Those rocks out there are the only grave I have to visit. Do you know it's seventeen years tonight? I feel the same weight as I did that night."

Percy sighed and stood, arching his back. "No one blames you, Gil, especially Ada. You didn't know that she was on board, coming home early. Take this gift. Next time they won't ask and you'll be out of here without a pension. That medal is about all used up."

The squeal of the pump handle filled the kitchen and water gushed from the nozzle into a large pot in the sink. Lifting the pot, Gil carried it to the stove and placed it on top to boil. "I have some dishes to do and you should head home before the storm rolls in," Gil said as he turned to face Percy. "You've been a good friend," Gil said and held out his hand. Shaking hands, the two men smiled at each other until Gil said, "Come on, I'll walk you down to the dock. It will take a while for the water to boil."

Boots weaved himself between the lighthouse keeper's legs as Gil stood at the end of the dock to see his friend off.

Percy rocked with the dory as the waves built, a quick glance at the windsock showed that weather had turned as Gil had foretold. Grinning at his friend's skill with predicting the weather, Percy wrapped his piece of cord around the flywheel of his make and break engine, and with a practiced pull, brought the reliable motor to life.

With its steady putt-putt adding a percussion to the music of the ocean, Percy settled himself in the stern of his craft and looked up at his friend. "Promise me you'll think about it? It's a generous offer and Ada would want you to be happy. This might be your last chance."

"Yes, last chance. Safe travels," Gil said and waved to the retreating boat.

Percy shook his head, raised his own hand in farewell, and turned the bow of his dory into the tiny whitecaps of the incoming tide.

Once his lifelong friend was nothing but a blur in the distance, Gil reached down and scooped up the tomcat that stood by his side. "Come on, you old thing, let's go put our supper on a bit early, shall we? I have a feeling that tonight will be a long night." As Gil walked down the wooden dock, the first storm clouds appeared over the horizon.

Gil pulled the heavy cast-iron pot to the edge of the coal stove as the thick fish stew bubbled and threatened to overtake the sides of the pot. It filled the air of the kitchen with the rich scent of salt fish, potatoes, wild onion, and bittercress, while Boots laid within his basket near the stove, his nose twitching as every bubble burst.

"Have no fear, I'll save some for you," Gil said and popped open the glass jar of cloudberry jam Perry had stashed in the monthly grocery delivery. Inhaling the tart jam, a smile tugged at the corners of his mouth, but it turned into a worried frown as the wind outside rose in pitch and began rattling the wooden shutters. His treat forgotten, Gil placed the jam jar onto the table and stared at his wife's empty place across from him, her crimson shawl a wound that would not heal. "Just like that night," Gil said.

The steady clomp of Gil's footfalls as he climbed the spiral staircase to the lantern room was enough to wake Boots from his rest. The tabby leapt from his basket and chased after Gil and overtook him. Darting between the man's legs as he climbed, the cat soon outpaced the man. When Gil got to the top, he found the tabby grooming his whiskers and giving the man a look of indignation.

Catching his breath, Gil shook a finger at Boots that went ignored. "Don't give me that look. You were perfectly fine in your basket, though I expect you needed to burn off some of your supper," Gil teased the cat and scooped him up and placed him on the room's ledge. In short order Gil had the powerful light from the kerosene lantern above his head burning its steady bright yellow flame, the hiss of the fuel as it was consumed along with the mechanical clicking of the reflective mirror which broadcast the light 360 degrees sounded right to Gil. Rapping his knuckle against the metal reservoir told Gil that the tank was still over half full, without having to dip the tank. Opening the valve, the lighthouse keeper put himself to the fuel pump handle and, much like the pump in his kitchen below, drew kerosene fuel from the main tank into the working reservoir for daily use. Satisfied that he'd have enough fuel for the foreseeable future, he set to work cleaning the gallery's windows. As Boots made circuit after circuit around the narrow ledge, Gil set to work cleaning the glass with a mixture of vinegar and water applied with a balled up piece of newsprint.

As he cleaned the glass of never ending salt spray and dust that clung to it, his eyes never left the horizon as the storm increased in strength once again, the howling wind seeking to penetrate the gallery which was a beacon to any ships on the water on this treacherous night.

His chores completed, Gil remained in the lantern room leaning upon the ledge, a flask of tea and a pair of binoculars at his left elbow, and curled up Boots at his right, the cat's purring lost in the roar of the storm outside.

"The resemblance to that night has been with me all day, growing stronger with every breath. It's almost as if it's the same storm returning, coming back around like the mechanics that spin my reflector, Mother Nature on a cycle that only she understands. I swear that if I strain my eyes, I can see the outline of the *Burgeo* coming out of the storm," Gil said and froze. His eyes narrowed, and he leaned forward under his forehead rested against the thick glass. "Dear god, there are some poor souls out in the storm."

He flung out his left arm, knocked over his flask, startling Boots, and grasped the brass binoculars. Fingers twisted with a lifetime of labour struggled to adjust the focus of the lens until the scene out in the ocean sprang to life. A wooden vessel, wide beamed and with a large billowing stack, had been up in the storm and tossed around as if a toy in the hands of a giant.

"Turn you fools!" Gil shouted as he watched helplessly as the lumbering ship headed for the rocks at the point, the high waves slapping the ship as if steering it. Gil just watched in horror, his jaw clenched tight, as the ship struck the rocks, its bow pointing skyward like a sacrificial victim.

The binoculars thudded upon the ledge and wobbled, but Gil had forgotten them as he ran to the stairs and raced down, the tabby on his heels.

Rushing to the kitchen door, Gil threw on his oilskin coat and placed his hand on the door's metal latch, Boots crowding him to be the first one out. Feeling the swell of the storm outside and the one building within him, Gil fought against the tides of fate and released the latch.

Scooping up Boots, Gil placed the cat in his basket and hurried to the pantry and in second returned with a brimming bowl of cooling fish chowder. He placed it beside the basket, rubbed Boots' ears, and said, "Take care of yourself." Without looking back, Gil raced out of the lighthouse and into the storm.

The wave hit the side of the dory and only Gil's lifetime on the water saved him from being capsized. Wind slashed water against Gil's uncovered face and hands. The sting felt like razors slicing his skin.

Staining against the oars, Gil wished he had Percy's

make and break engine to assist him as he realized that he wasn't as young as he was the last time he rowed to a stricken vessel. Keeping the lighthouse and its beacon of light at his stern, Gil pulled upon the oars and only took quick glances over his shoulder at his goal. With sweat and sea water making it hard for his aching hands to keep their grip, Gil got within the lee of the wounded ship and risked a proper look. Wiping eyes that stung from salt water, Gil looked upon the ship and struggled to understand. While it was pitch black in the storm with only the rotating light of the lighthouse acting as his guide, Gil knew something was wrong with the ship. Part of him had noticed it from the warmth and safety of the lantern room but had told himself it was a trick of the storm, but now there was no mistaking it. It was faded.

Not the faded that resulted from time and weather on the harsh seas, but the faded of spreading too little cloudberry jam on a piece of toast. Some of the ship was distinct when the yellow light of the lighthouse struck it, but in other places, the light shone straight through as if the timbers were nothing but an illusion. It flickered and rippled with a faint blue light as if it wasn't sure it wanted to be there, or, as Gil thought, maybe it was in two places at the same time.

"No, not places," Gil said to himself, "but two times."

A moment later proved his theory as the rotating beam of light on shore struck the damaged bow of the ship and red painted letters spelling *Burgeo* jumped out. The ship his wife died upon, a ship never replaced.

"I'm coming, Ada!" Gil yelled and pulled on the oars.

Out of breath and every muscle complaining, Gil got his dory through the jagged rocks which had penetrated the *Burgeo* by riding the fierce waves. Timing it to the second as one of the storm's waves lashed through the rocks, Gil leapt from his dory with line in hand, and scrambled through the darkness up the slippery rocks. Boots slipped and sharp rocks dug into Gil's hands, but he tied a hasty line around a rock and hauled his dory up against the rocks, so the pounding waves wouldn't smash it to pieces like the splintered timbers floating around him.

Gil shivered within his oilskin coat and not from cold. The scene before him was just as it was seventeen years ago. Sea water rushed into the smashed bow of the ferry with each wave. But something was also missing that was here seventeen years ago. There were no signs of life. Memories of that night plagued his sleep for years, the roar of the coal boiler that laboured unchecked, the cries of crew and passenger, lights flickered, casting shadows that turned into monsters in his dream were absent. No injured cried out in fear. There was no thump of the coal boiler, only the sounds of the storm. The *Burgeo* was as silent as a grave.

Knowing somewhere on board was his long-dead wife, Gil climbed into the dark maw of the damaged ship and disappeared.

There were no lights within the damaged hull, but Gil found he could see.

A soft blue glow filled the air of the dark hold, not enough to read by, but memory filled in the details that the ethereal light hid. He looked into the pens where livestock in distress had been seventeen years ago, now only filled with a layer of straw that dissolved into mist when touched. Realizing that the boards under his feet had a give, as if turning to mud, forced Gil to hurry.

"Ada!" Gil yelled and raced up the canted livestock ramp, the rough handrail only a wavering image in places. Reaching the passenger deck, Gil raced down the narrow hallway and ignored the small cabins where seventeen years ago he gathered frightened people and led them to his dory and rowed them to safety. Now the doors stood closed and silent. He burst through the swinging door to the main deck and looked to the stern, where years past passengers and crew had struggled to get the unconscious captain into the life raft. Now the deck was empty and only the cresting waves flowed across the rear of the ill-fated ship. Each strike weakened the fragile bonds holding the vessel together.

Turning away, Gil looked to the bow of the ferry, the only place he didn't look seventeen years ago. Presenting like a whale breaching out of the water, Gil climbed up the incline on hands and knees. The rocking deck and the dissolving nature of the ship made it difficult, but he rounded the wheelhouse and saw his wife.

Where everything else was dull and muted, Ada was colourful and solid, a beacon on this fading ship. She was struggling to release the forward life raft, but the pitch of the ferry made it so that gravity was working against her.

"Ada!" Gil yelled again, but the howling wind took his words, and his wife didn't turn. Scrambling forward, he reached for her arm and relief flooded his heart as she felt as solid to him as his own body. She was wet, shivering, with her second favourite shawl wrapped around her shoulders, but she smiled with joy upon seeing her husband and Gil thought she never looked so beautiful.

"I knew you would come," Ada said, and kissed her husband.

Unlike him, the years had not touched Ada. It was like the past seventeen years hadn't happened to her. "That's because they hadn't," Gil said to himself in realization as he struggled to stand. Another wave from the storm struck the ferry, and the deck shifted again, chasing away all other thoughts but escape.

"Take my hand, Ada."

The journey back to the dory was like crawling through a collapsing mine. Timbers fell and blocked their path as water pushed against their legs as if trying to keep them on board the sinking ferry, but guided by the yellow light of the lighthouse, Gil and Ada made it to the hole in the bow.

Hand in hand, the pair jumped from the looming maw of splintered wooden teeth and made it to the rocks. Now the entirety of the *Burgeo* was glowing in blue flames as the ship flickered in and out of existence and Gil realized they had only escaped in time. Turning his back to the ship out of time, Gil helped Ada across the rocks and into his battered dory.

Born and raised on this shores like her husband, Ada fitted the oars into the oarlocks as Gil scrambled to undo the line. Gil pushed the dory from the punishing rocks and leapt on board as Ada pulled on the oars.

Moving with the storm's wind and waves, Gil relieved Ada at the oars and she huddled at his feet out of the worst of the slashing wind. As he strained upon the oars to distance themselves from the rocks, he saw the blue flames that clung to the *Burgeo* like a halo flash like lightning and, in an instant, the ferry had disappeared. When the beam of the lighthouse next passed the spot, there was no evidence of a shipwreck, only the waves beat against the rocks.

Gil couldn't spare any time to contemplate what just happened as the storm, unlike the *Burgeo*, was still here and threatening to capsize the dory with every wave.

Strain as he might, Gil struggled to turn them towards the yellow light of the lighthouse, let alone make any headway in gaining the shore, and he found himself spent.

"I don't know if I can make the shore, Ada!" Gil yelled over the wind. "I'm not a young man anymore."

Whether she heard her husband's words over the storm or not, Ada smiled and grabbed Gil's hand and motioned for him to join her. Gil pulled upon the oars until tears flowed but in the end he nodded and slid to the bottom of the dory and held his shivering wife.

"I'm sorry, Ada; something gave me this chance to save you and I can't. I'm not strong enough," Gil said into her ear, the scent of lavender he also associated with his wife filling his nostrils.

Ada's arm slipped inside his oilskin coat, and she pulled her husband close. "Foolish old man," she said teasingly. "We're together, that's all that matters. Now hold me close."

Throughout the night, the storm raged and tossed the dory upon the whitecaps, but Gil and Ada held each other, content that they were together again.

Dawn. Streaks of orange and red filled the morning sky, chasing away the last vestiges of the storm. The air was fresh. Whatever had ridden upon the storm had gone.

Boots padded down the dock to survey his domain, the brisk wind ruffling his tabby coat. Standing at the edge of the dock, the cat spied the familiar dory on the rocky shore, the boat resting upright among fresh driftwood and seaweed at the high water mark.

Picking his way along the shore, Boots came up to the dory, sniffed and walked up the out-flung oar and stared within.

Sitting in the dory's bottom was Gil, silent, motionless, and alone. Boot reached out a paw and tapped the man twice upon the shoulder. As he made to tap a third time, the cat paused, looked at the man and lowered his paw. Boots stared at Gil's lifeless face, and perhaps even understood the smile that graced the dead man's lips.

Facing the outgoing waves, the cat allowed the wind to play upon his whiskers before jumping down onto Gil's lap for one last nap with his friend.

Harrison Shimens

Harrison Shimens is an author from Guelph, Ontario. He is an English and History high school teacher who has lived both by the ocean in Newfoundland and South Korea. Previous short story credits include "The Shape" in an upcoming anthology published by Scare Street, and "Old Growth" in *Unsettling Reads*.

Red Bay

"You know, they were always alive when they started cutting."

A slug of rum, a thud against the salt-soaked wood of the bar. My intrigue grew only slightly faster than the knot in my stomach. "Nope, nope. Took far too long to kill 'em, so they just started cutting away. Right there in the ocean."

We sat close, the man and me. A drag, a sooty breath blew past my nostrils. Arctic air whistled through an open door as a loaded local stumbled out of the dimly lit tavern. The man's story clawed deep into my mind. Red rivers draining from monochrome colossi, their shrieks of pain a tortured concerto. Another shot of rum dulled the sound.

That's why it was named Red Bay, I've been told. From contorting bodies, massive flanks of blubber and flesh were rent, spilling hundreds of gallons of steaming blood into the cold north Atlantic. When the hunt was at its peak fervor, there could be hundreds of them in the bay. Blood pooling, stagnating for weeks before it was finally flushed out to sea.

"Can't imagine the sound of it. Must've been hard for

those men to bear," the elder reflected, ashen eyes on his empty glass.

I sat in a town that was on the precipice of ancient wilderness. The hotel was the only accommodation for the next two hundred kilometers. It was brand new, and the three-storey modern structure sat in opposition to the small boxes and mobile homes that the locals resided in. Being the only source of booze in the community, the clientele consisted mainly of locals who only came to drink at the bar.

The hotel was built to appeal to rich Americans who were helicoptered in and out for guided big game hunting, and there were currently a handful of them tucked into bed, eagerly awaiting their five o'clock wake up calls. Each morning at six, a blue and orange helicopter landed by my ground floor window, erupting the still morning into a flurry of dust and chaotic noise. Pudgy white men in camouflage scurry onto the helicopter and are shuttled out into the maze of pine trees and black spruce and horseflies. And every evening at eight, moose and brown bears would be loaded off along with them. Shot and killed by tourists out in the bush, butchered and frozen by locals in the basement of the hotel.

Another few hundred kilometers up the gravel highway was Red Bay, my destination. The raspy man sitting next to me informed me of the Bay's origins as a Basque whaling port, a community in the 1500s of hardened men with blood on their hands, looking to make a fortune to take back to their families in Spain and France.

"Why're you headin' up to Red Bay anyway?" the man asked. His large t-shirt ballooned over his gut, hardened by years of rum and retirement. Below his overgrown, silver eyebrows, one of his eyes was permanently shut. "That place has been a ghost town since…" he counted on his dark calloused fingers. "Must have been thirty years now! Province tried to resettle 'em, but everyone was already gone."

I contemplated indulging myself in the retelling of my story: a great grandfather lost in time, a twenty-something lost in life. After looking the man up and down, I kept it to myself. He had heard enough tales, by the look of it. I told the man that I had a claim to a portion of land.

Those silver eyebrows raised, and his working eye bugged out of its socket.

"A claim of land?" a deep laugh bellowed from the man. I felt glad that I could provide a local with some entertainment. "I don't know why you'd want a piece of land up that way. My advice to you would be this, boy," his hand on my shoulder was heavy, and the sweet scent of rum was perspiring from his blemished face. "Don't stay longer than you have to. Make your visit brief." As he finished, he slammed his glass down for emphasis.

The lump in my throat grew larger. "Why should I do that?"

He paused. Looking behind the bar, carefully searching for the right words. A haunted look touched the man's glassy eyes.

"Listen," he shot the bartender a look. Wordlessly, another glass of rum was in front of him. "I understand we all got our own El Dorado. The key is to know when to stop searchin' for it."

The rum was gone again, and this time the man was

gone with it. Only the slight clink of washing glasses broke the silence. Growing tired and dreading the slow drive toward Red Bay, I asked the bartender for one final drink. My eyes drifted above the bar, and an old poem caught my eye:

> *'Over the Mountains*
> *Of the Moon,*
> *Down the Valley of the Shadow,*
> *Ride, boldly ride,'*
> *The shade replied,-*
> *'If you seek for Eldorado!'*

Sleep came slowly in the squeaky hotel bed. The nearly full moon cast grasping shadows over my bed. A wolf howled in the distance, and later, a gunshot.

The heater in my car fought back the cold with a grovelling hum. Around me black spruce trees and boulders littered the frigid landscape. Abandoned woodpiles, lobster traps, and dog sleds were piled along the road. They looked like abandoned shrines to industry, final vestments of humanity. The closer I drew to Red Bay, the fewer remnants of civilization resided on the sides of the highway. Those haunted altars trees receded with the trees, and the land became barren, as if all living things beside moss and lichen knew to stay away. Some things didn't belong in Red Bay. But I felt drawn to the place, like I had been caught in the gravitational pull of a planet. Or a black hole.

I continued down that long highway. I passed a sign: *Red Bay 150.* Time drifted slowly, ambling as if to give me as much of an opportunity to turn around as possible. The land was time's ally in this exercise, as the desolate landscape bore into my skull like a dull screw. But it wasn't enough to keep me away.

Two large steel arms adorned with orange and red lights guarded the entrance to the village. *When lights flashing, highway closed*, it read. The arms were rusty and looked as if the last time they had been functional was generations ago. The thought of being trapped out here in a storm came to my mind, and the words of that old man began to make a little sense. Being from the island, I knew bad winters, but not like what I had heard from the Big Land. Luckily it was still a few months before this part of Labrador could expect any real snowfall. I wore this thought like shining armor as I navigated the tight gravel road leading me into Red Bay.

Saltbox houses lined the rocky shore of the harbour, while boney fishing flakes and caved in sheds jutted out over the turbulent water. The icy waves battered the red earth, chiselled it into daggers. Out to sea, a patch of fog was forming and drifting along the water. Slowly driving through the town, dozens of ramshackle homes sat hunched like old corpses. Their bright pinks and blues and greens were faded, their doors unhinged, their windows shattered. Some looked as if they had been razed to the ground, leaving behind a splintered skeleton of lumber.

It wasn't long before I had found the saltbox of my own. Stepping inside the two-storey yellow box, the wood groaned in the blistering wind. Pungent warm air welcomed me to a home frozen in time: laundry left in a wicker basket, a pan on the wood burning stove, an open can of beans left to rot.

Obviously, the tenants had left in a hurry, but the question of *why* raised my heartbeat and a hot flow of curiosity coursed through my veins. The rush of history, of heritage, of facing the ghosts of my ancestors pulsed through my veins, and I felt like a leashed dog with a bloody steak placed just beyond my grasp. Then I lost control.

I regained sentience to opened cupboards, drawers thrown about, and furniture flipped. The paintings were torn off the wall, frames snapped to pieces. The yellow feather mattress was tattered, mouse droppings spilled across the floor like pebbles. Books, untouched for decades, fell apart as I frantically turned through them. This home that I had travelled so far to get to didn't even last ten minutes.

By the time I was finished, the house looked as if it had been ransacked. Guilt cooled me as I caught my breath, and fear set in. Throwing open the front door, I vomited up my previous meal of beefy jerky and soda. It steamed in the cool October air.

The sun was already starting to set. What just happened? It felt like I had become someone else or a piece of me that had been dormant had rose up and took control. Before I searched the rest of town, I decided to make my bed up for the night and rest.

My foot pushed down on the pump to inflate my air mattress. Its bellowing sounded like a massive lung at work. The wind had picked up and finishing with the air mattress I began to feel the chill full-on. Anticipating this, I had purchased wood from the hotel before I left. Leaving the house to get it from my car, I noticed how still the bay had become under the waxing moon. The water was only a few feet from the base of the house which produced a gentle lapping against the dilapidated wooden stage. It was comforting like a lullaby, and I found myself stepping closer to the edge of the bay as I listened. In my entrancement, a far away lonesome cry, a forlorn song, carried by the tranquility of the glassy surface of the water.

A blast of wind almost threw me off balance. The hypnotic sound of the water lost its effect on me, and something caught my eye. On the horizon, the thicket of fog had become a forest, probably twenty kilometers out. It would be here sometime during the night, and if I was lucky, would be gone by morning. Fumbling with the wood to bring it inside in one trip, the wind pushed the fog closer.

Opening the stove, ash blew into my face from the vent. At least I knew the vent worked. As I reached the first log into the stove, I noticed something covered in ash: a book. It had a rusty red binding, its pages yellowed and crisp with age. Inside the cover, delicate handwriting: *Erma*. My great-grandmother. The clue I must had been searching so frantically for.

As the fire roared across the room from my air mattress, I laid down in relative warmth and opened the old tome. The majority of the book was used as a tracker for her allowances, and to keep track of her egg sales. I read about her in my research at the archive. She had been an Inuit woman from Nain who married my great-grandfather after he had been up there for work. At least, that was my working theory. She disappeared along with my great-grandfather. Lost in time. The last remnant of her in my hands.

Breezing through the pages in hopes of finding the answers I was looking for, I turned to the last few entries:

October 25, 1901

Cold let up. Anthony out to fetch vegetables from the garden. Must let Brie know about quant. of potato. Fog out in the bay. Whales? Anthony may be seeing things. No whales in bay for hundred years or more. Oil could be sold and used if men hunt them.

See Brie after supp once veg count finished.

56 potato. 43 carrot. 17 turnip. 15 pumpkin.

Brie not home, queer behaviour. Walking home, I thought I heard her calling me from the other side of the bay. Across the fog. Could take a walk up Tracey Hill tomorrow, talk to Seamus.

October 26, 1901

6 egg breakfast, 2 potato

Fog moving from bay into town. I can hear Anthony's whales out in the fog.

Tracey Hill empty. Seamus gone and house a mess, fire smouldering. Looking for Brie after dinner. I am nervous and I do not want to look at the bay I do not know why.

Brie still gone. Anthony split his foot chopping wood. Not good but he does not seem worried. Not enough wood tonight. At least the fog takes away the chill of the night.

October 27, 1901

5 egg breakfast, 1 onion, 1 potato

Going to see if Brie is home. Will borrow supplies for Anthony's foot if she is there or not. Anthony keeps tearing off fresh bandages and he is telling me not to worry but I am worried. Praying for Brie and Seamus.

Anthony gone when I got home. Going to Pinware tomorrow if he does not return.

October 28, 1901

No breakfast.

Slept alone. Thought I heard Anthony outside through the night. His boots were wet. Going to Pinware but can not find axe, pony gone too. Heard a scream from the bay. Brie? Fog too thick to see.

Fog is nearly gone and couldn't sleep through the screaming and laughing.

Everyone is gone and the Bay is turning red. Black masses in the water. Whales? Is everyone out on a hunt? Can't go to Pinware. Waiting for Anthony.

October 29, 1901

Whales over the house last night. I could hear them. Fog is gone now. Bay is red and more are floating. Too small to be whales. Seal? Anthony's rifle still here. Going to the bay.

Anthony was tangled among the rocks and very pale. Tried to bring him back but his body was not transportable. Many more in the bay and could not find another soul in town. I fear my tears will ruin this book. I must go to Pinware tonight.

The entries stopped there and as the wind rattled the thin glass windows, it carried a whisper, pushing the fog on the horizon into Red Bay. Eyes wide, I stared into the flames of my fire with the book open in my hands until the October moon peaked in the bitter air.

My attention was pulled to the floor. A painting that had been flung off the wall earlier. Overcast skies speckled with gulls, a ravaging black sea. Plopped right in the centre were six men in a whaler. Grim faces, lashed red by the wind, armed with harpoons. In the foreground, a mass of black flesh breeched the surface of the violent waves. A gust of wind shook the saltbox and for a moment I felt as if I had been launched into the painting. Wool clothes and a cap, soaked in salt water, blasted by the gales.

I felt the ocean spray, I felt the ferocious wind, I felt the lust of the hunt.

My ancestors, settlers on this land, putting themselves through hell. And for what? *We all search for our own El Dorado.* The words of the old man, ripped from the poem, crept through my mind.

Darkness fell over the room and the cold seeped in as I let the fire die.

The cold woke me just before dawn. My toes were blue, and I shivered uncontrollably. I knew better than to let the fire go out at this time of year, yet here I was with nearly frostbitten feet. The painting sat on the floor in the corner, the gaze of those six whaling men fixed on me. A prolonged wail from the bay sent me out of bed, tripping over my numb toes. Through the window there was only gray. Flowing mists, hiding the surface of the bay. Was somebody out there?

My wool socks sat dejected over a chair near the fire. I fumbled around, inserting my thawing toes inside the socks, and then those socks inside my boots.

Outside, the atmosphere was on the verge of snow. Chilled crystalline formations melted on my skin. Thinking about a snowfall brought to mind those long metal arms on the highway, snow drifts making the drive back impossible, and being stuck in Red Bay. I calmed myself by repeating out loud that snow wasn't expected in the forecast.

"But neither was this fog," I retorted. I was right that it would blow through during the night, but wrong that it would be gone by morning.

The old wooden buildings looked like the decaying corpses of giants. Shivering, I added another layer of wool beneath my jacket. It felt unnatural and itched my skin at the neck, so I took it off and decided to deal with the cold. I figured that it would warm up as I walked.

Powerful gusts of wind howled past my ears and nearly took the cap off my head. Long, green grass thrashed wildly on the side of the gravel road. It hadn't even been a kilometer before I found a house that wasn't completed blown apart: a solidly built saltbox right on the edge of the bay, not that I could see it through the fog. Only the sweet sound of water lightly lapping against the jagged rocks let me know it was there. The north Atlantic in all of its icy glory and malice, thousands of kilometers of nothingness, right at my feet and I'd have no idea if it wasn't for that sound.

The door was locked but it didn't last long. It was a house very similar to the one I resided in. Same furniture, same old wood stove, but less decorative pieces. No paintings. Two other major differences: there was no second floor here, and right in the centre of the main room, was an open crawlspace door hung open like a broken jawbone, an old wooden ladder descended into the darkness below.

Was I really going down there? I had hardly finished asking myself this question by the time I had managed to use my lighter to ignite some old fireplace matches. I was already halfway down the steps, feet working on their own.

Small wooden casks labeled *Right Oil* and *Sugar* and *Rum* were piled high in one corner of the room. Uncorking one of the barrels released a fishy smell that penetrated my lungs and made me cough. Using my wool hat as an impromptu gas mask, my makeshift torch illuminated the tiny rocky space. A rusty ice pick lay on the floor, and above it, carvings. Hacked into the wall were images of bulbous creatures, and stick people. Tiny stick people. Or were the creatures' behemoths? By the dancing light of my flame the images came to life, a flipbook movie. Monsters behind the stick people. Shepherds herding them. Herding them where? I brought my light closer, and touching the wall covered my hand in soot. Fractal patterns and ridges guided my blackened fingers along runic symbols.

My matchstick went out, but I remained, tracing the shapes in the darkness, the smell of the ocean rending my nostrils raw.

I have no memory of me leaving that cellar, only the memory of fire. Standing outside the broken front door. Missing lighter from my pocket. Black smoke whirling into the sky and mingling with the fog. Intense warmth on my hands and face. Above me, in the darkening gray, a high-pitch wail.

Was it getting dark already? Or had the ocean sent more fog? It didn't seem to matter; sight wasn't needed to guide me back.

Sitting by the fire with a cold can of baked beans, I was watched by the men on the boat. Silently mocking me, I could stand no more. I turned to face them for parley. Unseen, the moon rose high, and the fire dwindled.

Stubborn old men, they couldn't hear me. An ancient rage brewed inside me. Their wool caps, their scowling faces, their animalistic desire for blood. The more I learned about them, the more I hated them. By the time I had calmed myself enough to go to bed, my vocal cords were scratched and torn. Bits of canvas and dry paint lay strewn about the small room, only shreds clinging to the wooden frame remained.

The fire was long gone when I heard the first cry. Just outside of Red Bay, the sun should have just crested over the horizon. But inside Red Bay, inside the fog, there was no light yet. Somewhere in the grey abyss came a gentle moaning cry, it sounded like a tiny girl. Swaying between a song and a scream, she continued without taking a breath.

Another cry in unison, right outside the front door. The high-pitched whine barely sounded human, which somehow made it more beautiful than anything. My feet began to take small careful steps toward the door, no less blue than yesterday, but much nimbler. Before I opened the door, the sound drifted away, as if carried by the wind. There was silence for a while after that. Sitting back down, I opened another can of beans.

The newly constructed fire warmed my body, and I massaged the blood back into my feet. But some cold is permanent. It lingered in me, twisted, and tightened around my bones like a million tiny nooses.

As the hours passed in that tiny house by the sea, more voices came and went in the susurrating wind and fog. Beautiful songs flowed into the house and soothed my ears, then shrieks of pure agony pierced them. There were tortured screams so loud they were audible through the hands over my ears. Rocking back and forth by the fire, I thought maybe if I lodged burning sticks in my ears, it might stop the songs. Or maybe I could shove my head into the cast iron belly and shut the door. It'd be warm and might untangle the chill from my bones.

A window upstairs shattered, and my gaze was drawn away from the fire.

Cold air coursed through the house, and loose paper and canvas were let loose into a flurry. Looking back into the fire for a moment, nausea welled in my stomach.

Up the creaky narrow staircase, milky mist flowed into the house like molasses.

The fog had found a way in.

Approaching the window, I could see that the fog had let up, as if it had begun to drain away as it poured into the house. Through the clearing, the bay was visible.

A crimson tide frothed against the rocky shoreline. For a moment I looked back into the house and saw ruby droplets and smeared rusty footprints. It seemed that I had sliced my foot on glass and hadn't even noticed.

The calls continued above me and protruding my head outside the window — a ghostly colossus swam through the fog. Primordial warmth coursed through my veins. Each beat of my heart carried it deeper into my being. I could feel the cold chipping away. I was a block of marble and the entity above, my sculptor.

It swayed beautifully through the fog, singing an ancient ballad of life, death, and creation. How could a mortal be so honoured by one's shepherd? Why did it choose me? Warming tears flowed down my face and I wheezed through clenched teeth. A swell of voices from the bay called to me now.

They were in the water too! I could see them, hundreds of blubbery backs breaking the surface of the ocean, each one majestically frolicking in the world below. Massive, pitchforked tails beat the surface of the water, sending a pink froth into the air.

They called to me. They told me it was my time, and I was outside.

Standing at the shore.

Warm, red water splashed my toes and invited me in. Above me in the sky, below me in the sea: celestial entities, gods, and they were here for me! Who was I turn away from the herd? It was my time.

My last thought before dunking my head below the waves was the faces of those horrible men on the boat. If only they could see me now.

Taking a moment to listen to one final song, I took my final breath and joined the shepherds below the waves.

Daniel Windeler

Daniel Windeler hails from Happy Valley Goose Bay and is a wildlife biologist who has worked both the offshore of the Atlantic and deep in the forests of the province.

His first published story was "Freeson's Leap" in *Pulp Science-Fiction from the Rock*. He brings with him his next titanic tale 'Wave Bound.'

Wave Bound

Even though it was late June, I felt the morning chill coming off the water. St. John's harbour always had a knack for making what should have been a cool summer day start out as cold as possible. It was a little after eight o'clock as I stepped out of my car, coffee in hand and my laptop bag hung to my side. Locking the door, my gaze fell on the bustling streets of the downtown across the harbour. Even though it was Sunday, the streets were full of employees and bankers looking for parking, and students from the university coming down to eat at one of the cafes.

Usually, I would be with them, getting dressed a little after nine and heading down for waffles by the water with my friends. Sunday is when I catch up with them, get a few errands done in the afternoon, and prep some meals for the week. But today I was called in for a meeting and told to be prepared for it to take all morning, maybe all day if the findings weren't good. But I had to be prepared for days like this to happen when a death needed to be investigated.

I stood in front of the gatehouse, waiting for a tired

looking guard to come back to the window. A man in his forties sat down at a desk and pulled the window open.

"Name and reason?" he said, his bay accent faint but noticeable.

"Alex Keller, Occupational Health and Safety officer." I pulled out my driver's licence and my provincial government ID, placing them on the windowsill. The guard looked them over, bushy brow furrowed as he read the government ID. I didn't really look the part of a government employee at the moment, wearing sneakers and jeans along with my collared shirt. But I was told to come casual for this, as one of the reasons we were doing this on the weekend was to make the employee feel as comfortable as possible.

"Alright, wait by the gate and someone will come out to show you inside." He handed back the government ID but kept my licence; I would get that back when I came through. I strung the GUEST card across my neck and waited by the gate.

Standing in the chill, I opened my bag and pulled out a folder. I just wanted to review the incident one last time before the interview. Four nights ago, one of the commercial fishing vessels was caught in a storm off the coast of southern Labrador. The *Laura's Luck* had their nets out when the storm hit, and in fear of the nets getting tangled and cut, they tried to pull them in before it got worse. During the clean up, a young crewman by the name of Marcus Bryce fell overboard. The storm raged until midday, and Marcus' body was never recovered. The call of what occurred came back, and *Laura's Luck* along with two coast guard vessels searched for the body, but to no avail. The provincial office had been notified of the death and the investigation began, with Occupational Health and Safety Officers interviewing each of the fishermen as to what happened.

Every interview went as to be expected with a union rep present and all questions answered — all but one. I pulled out the notes made about Eric Clark, a twenty-three-year-old apprentice fish harvester originally from Rocky Harbour. When he was interviewed, he refused his union rep and was unhelpful, if not outright hostile, to my supervisors. That is why I was called in on a Sunday in jeans, to try to make him as comfortable as possible in order to get his side of the story. Being a junior officer myself, only having three years on the guy, my boss thought I might be more relatable.

I didn't know how this was going to go down; one of my first fatality interviews and I looked like I was ready for a garden party. Everything about this felt odd, unprofessional even. I didn't know how I was supposed to make this Eric guy comfortable when even I didn't feel it.

The sound of the electric gate opening brought me back to the world. A portly man wearing a safety vest stood on the other side.

"Follow me. Eric's waitin' for ya' in tha' office up 'ere," he said with a grunt. All business. I got that a lot from the older workers since I joined OH&S. We were never around when they started, and now because of government regulations, we were crawling all over their worksites like fleas, or that's how they saw it. I nodded quietly and followed him over to a two-storey building by the water. A few faces turned to watch me enter, some confused as to why some civilian was past the gate. I could tell who knew why I was there; they glared at me, mumbling something under their breath. They thought I was there to pester Eric, poke and prod him until we found someone to blame Marcus' death on, bothering a poor kid who just lost a friend. I acted like I didn't notice and continued to follow the guy into the building.

Down a hallway and to the right and my escort stopped in front of a door that said "Kitchen" on the sign. He pointed at it and gave another grunt. I thanked him, but he was already on his way out, so I didn't know if he heard me. I rolled my eyes and opened the door.

Eric barely looked up when I entered the room; he was hunched over one of the tables, playing with the spoon in his coffee cup. Even though he was wearing a ball cap, I could see the heavy bags under his eyes; he probably hadn't slept since the storm.

"Hello, Eric, my name is Alex Keller, I'm here to ask you—"

"I know why you're here!" his words almost came out as a snarl; the glare from his green eyes was piercing. I raised a hand as I went to sit at the table across from him, putting my bag down by my feet. He didn't argue with me when I sat, so that was something.

As I leaned over to rummage through my bag, I took my bearings of the room. The large window with a view of downtown was different for me. Usually, we did these interviews in someone's office or a windowless room, somewhere where we could control the distractions, keep the employees' attention. But having it in the kitchen was to make Eric feel like this wasn't an interrogation.

I kept an eye on Eric as I sifted through the bag, but the guy's focus went back to the spoon the second I sat down. Constantly stirring, the clinking of the metal against the mug lightly echoed through the room. I wasn't sure if this was some sort of nervous tick or whether he just wanted to fill the silence in the room; maybe this was his only physical outlet for his frustration, other than climbing over the table and clobbering me. I wanted to say it was one of the former options, but that snap when I came in....

His gaze fell onto the folder I pulled out, but he frowned when I put my phone onto the table and opened an app.

"What's that for?" Eric's question was thick with venom; his fingertips turned white as he gripped that spoon harder.

"A recording is always done at these meetings. It's mainly for your sake," I jumped in before he could protest. "Since you don't want a union rep in the meeting, you can make sure you know I didn't lie or make any accusations towards you." I tried to reassure him, but I could see Eric's shoulders tense up when I mentioned the recording. Why was he so worried about others hearing this? Was he afraid of being accused of being a nark? Eric's eyes darted back and forth from me to the phone, trying to find a good reason to argue against the recording. But he stayed silent, his unshaven jaw set as he clenched his teeth.

"So... where would you like to start on the night of the storm?" I tapped my phone and the recording started.

"I didn't see anything," were Eric's first words, leaning in close to the phone so it was clear. I just sighed and opened the file.

"Okay, then how about we talk about your duties on the night of the incident," I proposed, already knowing them from the file. Eric just looked at me, a little confused. "What was your job that night?"

"I was helping the captain, why?" His eyes narrowed. He didn't really know where this line of questioning was going and was waiting for some sort of trap.

"Okay, but what did that entail?"

"Regular duties. Listening to the captain." He finally sipped the coffee he was playing with all this time, looking for a little break. I just sat quietly, waiting for him to elaborate, and he knew that. Finally, he snorted, "The job was Officer on Watch! I keep track of the navigation and look out for anything around the vessel we could hit."

"So, you look ahead, just to make sure there's not another boat out in the water."

"Yes! Among other jobs!"

"So, you had a good view of the deck that night?" It was more of a statement than a question because we both knew it was true. Eric just looked at me wide eyed, finally letting go of that bloody spoon and letting it rest by his mug.

"Well, I spend a lot of time looking at the computers, GPS, and stuff. Also the stern. I might not be paying attention to the deck. Too busy, especially in a storm!" The excuses came flooding out of his mouth, all the places he'd be staring at instead of the deck. But I just shrugged.

"Yes, but you'd still see the deck from the bridge, where the watch was. Also, you'd turn in the direction of any commotion if an incident occurs, right?" Eric didn't respond. "Right?"

"…Yes." It was little more than a mumble, but confirmation all the same.

"Alright. So, the storm hit, the nets were out. They needed to be pulled in. Tell me what happened next."

"The crew went out and started pulling the nets in. They used the winch and got to work on getting them on deck and secured. Some of them had fish inside so it took a while. I couldn't do much because I was on the bridge with the captain," He listed it off quickly before taking a sip of his coffee, hoping that I would be satisfied with that answer.

"Tell me about Captain Morris."

"What about him?"

"How did he get hurt?" Not only did Marcus die during the storm, but Captain Morris had broken his leg in two places. The other crewman said he had fallen down the stairs on deck when Marcus went overboard, but I wanted to hear what Eric had to say. Unfortunately, very little.

"He fell."

"Okay, but where?"

"On deck."

"Why was he on deck, Eric?" I was firm with that question. I was getting nowhere slowly, and comfort be damned, I was going to have to start pushing Eric if we were going to figure out anything.

"Because of the accident! Because Marcus fell overboard and when you're a captain, you kind of worry about that!" Eric's voice rose to a shout at the end, the full weight of his frustration and exhaustion now showing in his face. "Why are you asking me all this? You know what happened in the storm! Everyone else told you!"

"I want to know your side of the story, Eric." I spoke calmly, not matching his volume. While I might not have looked the part in that moment, I was still a professional.

"What, so you can see what I say different?! Looking for someone to pin all this on because Marcus died?! It was an accident! Everyone said that!" He rose to his feet, fists balled up and hanging by his waist.

"Yes, everyone did say that, but I want to hear what you saw." That was the problem; everyone did say that: *exactly* that. My supervisor and coworkers interviewed the whole crew, and every single one of them just told the same story. It might not have been word for word, but when reading them together, the similarities couldn't be ignored. Too many similar phrases used and said around the same time in the story. Everyone saw Marcus unbuckle his harness to grab for a rope, even the captain.

It all sounded staged, too prepared in advance for the interviews. Every single one of them said what needed to be said so no one was reprimanded.

Everyone but Eric.

"Well, I didn't see anything special. Marcus was out helping everyone, and he took his harness off. He shouldn't have done it and he knew better but he took it off!" Eric was yelling now. I started to wonder if anyone was listening in the hallway. If he got violent, would someone rush in to stop him? Remembering the glares that I got coming in, I realized probably not. I hoped my nervousness didn't show as I sat with my hands on the folder, Eric still standing over me.

"So, Marcus was out with the rest of the deckhands to

work on the nets?"

"Yes!"

"Why?"

"Because he works on the deck!" Eric was screaming now.

"No, he doesn't. Marcus was hired on to work on the engine." Flipping the folder open, I pulled out the crew listings with everyone's positions. It was the file that was copied from the crew manifesto and sent to the port authority when they originally left port a few weeks ago. "This is from the original because the manifesto given to us after the accident was altered."

Eric froze, his mouth agape but completely silent. He looked down at the copy of the manifesto like it could explode at any second, hands shaking.

"There was no reason for Marcus to be on deck during the storm. The rest of the crew lied about him being a deckhand and I want to know why." My eyes locked with Eric, whose mouth was moving but he couldn't think of anything to say. There were no more excuses, I caught him in the lie and there was nowhere to run. "Tell me what happened the night of the storm, Eric."

With that, he finally collapsed back into his chair, shoulders slouched as he stared down at the paper with a dejected look.

"You aren't going to believe me…."

"Try me." The anger and suspicion from before were all gone. His lips fumbled for a few seconds before he finally let out a deep sigh. Gently, he reached over and turned off the recording. I wanted to object, but he just raised his hand.

"I don't want anyone else to hear this," Eric said softly. There was a pleading look in his tired eyes. It was hard to believe that this was the same rowdy witness I started the interview with. I was taken aback but gave in to his request. Everything about this interview was abnormal anyway so might as well take this off the books. I was finally getting somewhere at least. I waited patiently for Eric to get his thoughts in order, and with a ragged groan, he finally spoke.

"The storm hit fast. We still had the nets out. Usually, we would just sail out of the storm before bothering with the nets, but we already had a catch. Tugging that weight for so long risked breaking them. So, the crew was out on deck, harnessed to the deck poles. The captain and I were on deck. I was to keep an eye on navigation to make sure we didn't go off course, and the captain was at the wheel. Marcus was on the bridge, on call just in case any of the sensors went off." Eric's face contorted into a fearful scowl before he continued,. "It was after we pulled the net up when we saw it."

"Saw what, Eric?"

"The lights… the lights in the water." Eric's shoulders tightened from a shiver, his face fell to his coffee again, which was chilled by this point.

"What do you mean by lights?"

"I mean what I said. There were lights in the water." Eric looked up but the statement wasn't said with any snideness. He looked me directly in the eyes, gauging my reaction to that statement before explaining more. "I never saw anything like it before, but there was this glowing… *stuff* in the water. With the storm raging, it was hard to see what they actually were, but they glowed bright green, then blue. There was like a dozen of them, on either side of the boat, just below the waves."

"Glowing lights? Like bulbs or beacons?" This had taken a weird turn. Truthfully, I was expecting Eric to tell me someone was drinking on the job, or the captain sent Marcus out to work in unsafe conditions. But… underwater lights? I wanted to call Eric out on this story, but that look he gave me… the turn in his attitude. Something stopped me and I let him explain further.

"Yeah, one second they would be round like balls and then they'd grow skinny like a snake." He was pleading now: with the hurt in his eyes, you'd think I had called him a liar, but maybe my own eyes were saying it. "I know what it sounds like, but I'm telling you the truth! There was glowing stuff in the water around the boat!"

"Was it those shrimp or plankton that excrete that glowing blue liquid sometimes on the coast?" I was looking for some kind of explanation for his glowing lights, but Eric just shook his head.

"No, I saw that stuff on the west coast once. Pics of that were on the news. This wasn't like that. These things were as big as my head, one even bigger. Trust me, if this was shrimp, I'd know it!" But I didn't trust him. He'd started to look a little manic when he explained the glowing bulbs under the sea. But I just gave a nod to let him continue.

"So they showed up about an hour into the storm. We were the first to notice on the bridge 'cause the rest of the crew was working on the net. We called out on the radio, and when the crew looked at the lights… that's when they started to change." The last part was no more than a whisper, and to my shock, Eric's hands were shaking on the table.

"Change?" I asked and Eric just nodded.

"Yeah, it was like someone gave them a good hard smack upside the head. Even from the bridge, I could see this dumb look on their faces. The second they saw the lights, they went dumb and funny. They started to wander away from the net and over to the rails. One by one, the whole team was walking to the edge of the deck. They tried to climb the rails, but the harnesses wouldn't let them get any further. They… they tried to jump off the boat!"

"Some of your crew tried to kill themselves?!" Because that's what that was. Days from land and in the middle of a storm, it was suicide. Anyone over the rail that night was a goner; Marcus could attest to that.

"Not some, all of them! Every deckhand tried to throw themselves overboard!" Eric was almost shouting now, a mix of fear and relief flooded his face, as he was finally able to tell someone his tale. "I don't know why they did it, but the captain started screaming over the radio, but none of them cared." It was then that he noticed his shaking hands. Balling them up in fists was futile; they continued to shake and Eric let out a mournful shudder. "They… they just didn't care anymore…."

"Why would they do this? Your crew knows the risk. Why every single one of them?"

"It was the lights! I don't know what they are, but the second they saw them, that was it. They made a B-line for the rail and tried to jump off. Their harnesses got tangled and poor Whalen was getting stepped on by Carl, but they didn't care! They just kept tugging, reaching out for the water from the railings and they ignored all the radio calls!" Eric's gaze was darting around, staring at some unseen vision, the memories of that terrible night replaying over his face.

"We could see the lights from the bridge, but we weren't going after them like the rest of the crew." Eric shuddered. "Not yet anyway. When they refused to answer, Marcus ran over to the door and went to yell at the lot of them. The moment he stuck his head out to the storm, he was the same way."

"Like the rest of the crew?" I asked, but Eric just balled up his hands and looked like he was on the verge of tears.

"His body went slack, and that dumb look went on his face. I could see it from the window and knew he was like the others. He then made his way for the deck, without a coat or a harness." The shaking subsided and Eric gave heavy breaths to calm himself. "That's when the captain went after him. The captain yelled out to Marcus to get back inside. He leaned out and grabbed him by the shoulder and tried to pull him back in. But Marcus was a big guy. He just lurched forward and dragged the captain out on the bridge. I don't think he tried to, but nothing was stopping him then."

"Is that when the captain broke his leg?" I couldn't believe I was asking this, that I was going along with this story! It was so ridiculous, magic lights doing... doing what to them? Hypnotizing? Taking control? The absurdity of this... but Eric's face.... Just looking at him told me that whatever he said, he believed it to be fact!

"Marcus' tug pulled him off balance and he slipped on the wet flooring. Went down the stairs and caught his leg in the railing, got tangled up and broke it so bad that the bone stuck out." Eric just shook his head, eyes closed as he retold the incident. "He never screamed when it happened, not a single peep. The lights had him by then. Bone sticking out and twisted and all he did was reach out for the lights. That's all that saved him."

As I listened, the outcome of this tale finally clicked in. A chill ran over my back, and I waited for Eric to look up at me again.

"The captain's leg was broken, and the crew had harnesses. All but Marcus." Eric was shaking again, face scrunched up to hold back the sobs. But I pushed, I needed to hear him say it. This couldn't be left unsaid. "Eric, did Marcus willingly jump off the boat?"

"It was so casual. He just walked across the deck, slipping past the tangled crew, soaked by the rain, but he was so calm. I think because he *knew* nothing was stopping him is why he wasn't pulling like the rest." Tears ran down his cheek freely now. "He just… climbed over the rail and jumped off. He hit the water and didn't come back up."

I let out a breath that I didn't realize I was holding, but it was ragged and hoarse. My heart was pounding as I watched Eric sob on the other side of the table. I didn't want to believe him. The rational side of me wanted to say that this was some defence mechanism in response to watching a tragedy. But I couldn't deny this sobbing man his trauma, nor the peculiarity of the rest of the crew and their drone-like explanation of the fake events. I wanted to say he was lying, but I couldn't bring myself to do it.

"When did the lights stop? When Marcus jumped?"

"They didn't, not until the storm passed." Eric bent over and put his head in his hands. When he rose, I could have sworn he aged years. "I was all that was left, everyone else was trying to free themselves to jump off the edge. I took the wheel once the captain fell; someone had to steer the boat in the storm." He sounded so haggard, so broken. "I was left there for hours, watching my crew try to kill themselves, and I couldn't do anything to help them. We were so turned around by that point that I didn't know which way to steer the boat out, just to keep it from tipping. I was alone on the bridge until morning... watching the lights from behind the glass, and my friends fighting the only thing that was keeping them alive... the captain's leg was a state by the end of it, tearing at the railing. He won't walk on it right for years...." The memory took over again and Eric sobbed into his hand.

The thought of being trapped alone on that boat with the lights of the storm and the mesmerized crew until morning was too much. Looking down, I realized my own hands were shaking and I quickly clasped them together, willing them to cease. No wonder Eric was traumatized; the image of Marcus climbing over the rail to his death was burned into his mind. It was Eric's voice that brought me out of the horrific image.

"When the storm ceased and the lights sunk back into the waves, I thought it was over. I called the coast guard for help and the rest of them seemed to come back to their senses. But when we met up with the coast guard, the captain told them that Marcus fell overboard because he took his harness off! Then, they all went along with the story, saying he was a deckhand. I went to say something but when the captain gave them the manifesto, they changed Marcus' job."

"Did they think no one would believe them?" I was still having trouble believing the whole tale, but Eric shook his head no.

"No. When I asked them after, none of them remembered the lights, or that's what they told me. I thought they were back to normal, but I was wrong." Eric's next words were but a whisper, as if he was afraid someone would hear us. "They don't care about Marcus or this investigation. All they want to do is get back to the ocean, as fast as possible."

"To get back to normal?"

"No, I think they are going back to look for the lights again." Eric just shook his head. He looked so tired; telling me this whole story took more out of him than I realized. If he collapsed right then, I wouldn't have been shocked. "Nothing but those lights matter now."

"If they aren't in their right mind, then we need to warn someone. I need to tell my supervisor." I fumbled with that. How the hell was I supposed to tell them about glowing lights in the water and mesmerized fishermen killing themselves? I looked back at Eric. "How am I supposed to tell them this without getting them all institutionalized?" Or myself, for that matter.

"I don't care if they don't believe me! I don't want your bloody approval to go back!" His voice arched high and he jumped to his feet, eyes bulging in fear. "I'm not going back out to sea, you can't make me!"

"Eric, wait. I'm not going to make you. Just wait. We can figure so—" The two of us nearly jumped out of our skin when my phone buzzed. Damn, I forgot to turn it on airplane mode before the meeting. It buzzed on the table and my supervisor's number lit up the screen. Before I could say anything, Eric was already on his way to the door. I reached up, but he was already out of the room before I could protest. Cursing under my breath, I answered the phone. "Yes?"

"Alex, what did you find out from that Eric kid?" There was a hoarseness to my boss' voice that wasn't normal, as if he'd spent the morning yelling.

"Um, I was just finishing the interview when you called. The little I got out of the interview wasn't helpful." That was a lie I'd have to deal with later. I wasn't telling my boss over the phone about underwater lights.

"Well, I need something because the rest of them are gone!" my supervisor hollered. "They went to the docks sometime this morning and set sail! They know they're not supposed to leave! We can arrest the lot of them!"

"They don't care about that." The pit of my stomach went hollow, knowing exactly where they were going. "Tell the coast guard they are heading for the nearest storm."

"Storm? How do you know that? What did Eric tell you?!" My boss was nearly yelling through the phone now, and in the background, I could hear some more folks yelling.

"Not much, but that they are going to head for a storm, like the one Marcus died in. Sorry, sir, but I need to go." I hung up before he could object and ran down the hallway. But by the time I reached the entrance, I watched a car speed off into the city. I didn't need to use any investigative skills to realize that Eric was making a break for it.

I had been right in the end. By the time the coast guard set out to look for them, The *Laura's Luck* had headed straight into a storm about a day's sail from St. John's. The coast guard skirted the edge and only found them when the storm dissipated. It was morning when they came upon the vessel. bobbing on the waves. It was radio silence from the *Laura's Luck*, and when the guard finally pulled up beside it, they realized it was abandoned.

Not a soul was found on board, and the ship still held both emergency rafts. Even all the life jackets and float suits were accounted for. They looked for any sign of the crew, but none could be found. It was as if they vanished in the middle of the storm. But I knew better. It seemed they didn't even bother with the harnesses this time.

Like Marcus before them, the search for the missing crew was called off. I was interviewed later to figure out what I had learned from Eric. By the time they discovered the abandoned ship, Eric was already off the island, having bought a plane ticket for that very night. I left out as much as I could without sounding suspicious, having told them Eric was manic and unhelpful, even for me. After weeks of questioning, they gave up on it and ruled the whole disappearance as a tragic accident.

Sometimes, I think about that interview, about what I learned from Eric. I tried to contact him after the investigation, to update him on his old crew, but all I could find out was he moved to Fort McMurray with cousins, working in a new field. I shouldn't have been surprised by that, remembering those fearful eyes as he relived the night alone on the bridge. He moved as far away as he could from the ocean.

Sometimes I wonder, when I look out to the ocean, if Eric will ever come back. Probably not, knowing the wave bound lights are still out there, in the storms, waiting for the last member of the *Laura's Luck*.

Melissa Bishop

Born and raised in Mount Pearl, Bishop is a newcomer to the genre fiction scene in Atlantic Canada whose fantastic prose has taken the province's community by storm. Her work won three Kit Sora awards: July 2019 "Cycles", September 2019 "Huntress of the Woods", and May 2020 "Brightest and Best". Additionally, she has placed numerous other times.

Writing about her story "The Photograph" in *Pulp Science-Fiction from the Rock*, R. Graeme Cameron of Amazing Stories wrote: "This is a classic SF tale... Possibly a reminder that things aren't always what they seem."

Bishop describes herself as a loyal Tolkien fan who enjoyed reading about different mythologies as a child. She currently works as a high school teacher, teaching at the same high school she attended in her youth. She started writing when she was very young and honed her skills in high school, when she started a pen pal friendship that has lasted for over seventeen years, writing stories back and forth to each other.

In 2022 she releases her first solo prose work, *The Fairies of Foggy Island*, with sculptor Nicole Russell and photographer Kyle Callahan.

Battlin' Blue Men

The limo, dusted with dirt road, pulled up on the uneven pavement of Ullapool Port, a small plod of land that jutted out into Loch Broom like an upward thumb. Dommie Dee looked dismally out at the wharf from his tinted windows. He hadn't left the city since his rise to fame. He had sworn never to enter a small dive town again, not if they paid him a million bucks. If only he wasn't broke.

"This is the stop, sir," the driver announced abruptly, disrupting Dommie from his woes. The ship floated before them, rust stains trailing along its hull in long orange streaks. It was an older vessel, worn from good use on rough seas. Dingy metal containers lined the deck in neatly stacked rows. It was a cargo ship, which made Dommie frown further. He had been expecting a private yacht or at the very least a cruise ship. This was a floating dumpster in comparison and served only as another reminder of his plummet from popularity.

Dominic Devlin, now known almost exclusively as Dommie Dee, had risen to celebrity status when his local rap battles found their way onto the internet, turning him into an online sensation. New to the music biz, Dommie Dee signed the first contract he was handed and then went on a spending spree. His debut album hit it out of the ballpark. The fans amassed as his popularity skyrocketed with worldwide shows, celebrity award ceremonies, and lavish parties. Dommie Dee led a luxurious life during this time — his popularity practically demanded it. He had never seen this kind of money before. It flowed like a fountain that would never run dry — but run dry it did.

Two album flops, a few poor investments, and the fickle nature of social media stardom left Dommie with bills he could no longer afford. All his prospects dried up like dead grass. This was the last good gig his manager could get him and the details surrounding the job were foggy at best. There was a brief mention of Dommie's old days and his rap battles, but really it didn't matter. Dommie hadn't been given a choice. Do this job or drown in debt. What other option was there?

As Dommie stepped out of the car onto the gravelly dock, his driver retrieved a bag from the trunk and laid it at the rapper's feet. "Enjoy your trip, sir," the chauffeur said, his tone more apathetic than endearing. Watching the car drive off, Dommie found himself glad to be alone.

The media had dogged his steps during his days in the sun; he was almost thankful no one was here to witness his fall. As he turned towards the tarnished plank way, he saw a tall, slender man striding towards him. The sailor had a steady gait that, despite his slim frame, seemed suitable for uneven seas. His brown beard bushed about the edges of his chin and his eyes shone almost silver — overcast tinged with sunlight. His handshake was hearty like his laugh, which roared from his lips as he took hold of Dommie's hand and shook the rapper's willowy arm.

"The fella from the internet!" His voice rolled like thunder. "Pure dead brilliant, ye are! Mighty glad to meet ya!"

"Yea, that's me. Dommie Dee," the rapper replied, standing straight and trying his best

to look the part of an illustrious celebrity. "But this ain't a yacht. What exactly you got me out here for?"

"All in time, me lad. Let's get aboard and settled. Plane ride good? I imagine it was a wee bit long, coming from the States an' all." The man grasped Dommie's luggage and threw it over his shoulder. "First Mate Murdock Findley, at yer service!" The man's laugh boomed again as they mounted the plank onto the vessel. Stepping aboard, Dommie took a sweeping look over the situation on the ship. It wasn't pretty. There was hardly a crew member in sight, and those who shuffled about barely glanced at Dommie before scuttling off to some other task. They weren't the kind of swooning fans he had gotten used to. Again, he felt grateful for anonymity. Dommie followed behind as Murdock lumbered across the deck and down a steep staircase leading to a narrow hallway of small doors. Murdock kicked the third on the left wide and dropped Dommie's bag on the cramped cot of a tiny room. One small, solitary porthole gave a glimpse of the sea. It was damp and dark, like most of the ship appeared to be. Dommie was too bewildered, too desperate to protest his room, and Murdock's face was so warm that Dommie had a hard time feeling the discomfort of the place.

"Right, settle in and when yer ready, I'll be above

deck."

The rapper was left to look about his lodgings — no larger than the maid's closet in his once extravagant abode.

Dommie didn't spend much time below deck. Now keenly aware of the world he would exist in while on board, the young rapper settled his mind to find out the particulars of his performance as soon as possible, then get the job done, and get out of here. He rose above deck just in time to see the boat departing the dock, drifting off into the green-grey sea. There was something serene about the scene, and Dommie allowed himself a moment to imagine he was a simple sailor on the ship. That he'd never known fame. Before the obscene mansions and absurd lifestyle, Dommie had genuinely loved to rap. Sure, there wasn't much money in it, but Dommie had always been good at shaping words into rhythm and song. More than that — rapping was his passion. He loved it. Dommie had forgotten that somewhere along his pursuit of popularity. That mistake had led him here — adrift on the ocean. Lost and alone.

Murdock was on the bridge of the ship when Dommie found the man. The sailor's eyes were settled on the wide expanse of ocean before them, so he didn't see the young rapper at first. Beside Murdock stood a woman dressed in a thick woollen sweater that matched Murdock's own. A cap adorned her head, her black hair braided to the left side of her shoulder. She was, like her first mate, staring out at the grey day through the wheelhouse windows.

When Dommie cleared his throat to interrupt their vigilance, the woman turned. He registered surprise in her deep green gaze.

"So this is the lad ye got?" she said, her serious expression softening as she looked Dommie up and down. The sea churned beneath the boat, forcing Dommie to steady himself against the wall, "Ye didn' say he was so young, Murdock!"

"Don't matter. He's the best," Murdock retorted. The first mate stepped forward and wrapped one arm round Dommie's shoulders, gesturing his free hand towards the woman with black hair and green eyes. "This here is Aisla Findley, my Captain and wife. And Aisla — this be our hero! The most famous rapper to be found. Aren't ya lad?"

"The best of the best," the young rapper replied, trying to sound self-assured. "Now, tell me, what's this gig all about?"

Aisla blinked, her expression once more showing surprise. "He don't know?!" Aisla's tone turned dark and scolding, her arms crossed in disapproval as she set her eyes on Murdock. The man shrank at her displeasure. "Ye let this lad on our ship and *he don't even know why he's here*?!" Unease crept along Dommie's spine as Murdock's arm dropped slowly from the rapper's shoulders. Aisla's next words were a command. "We tell him now, Murdock. Now."

"Aye. Aye," Murdock replied, crestfallen. His grey gaze glanced at the few shipmates tending the cargo ship controls. Then, uncertain about discussing the matter before the crew, offered, "In our office then. Come on."

Murdock turned and gestured to a small door. A tiny room lay behind it, with only a desk, a few chairs, and one small flickering light. Maps lined the walls along with family photos. Like the rest of the boat it was drab and dusty, as if it had stood still for far too long. Aisla sat behind the desk, a table bolted to the floor, and gestured for Dommie to take a seat across from her. He obliged immediately. The small waves that shifted the floor made him nauseous on his new sea legs. Dommie wanted to keep as confident an air as he could and so was glad to get off his feet. Afterall, Aisla seemed skeptical of the rapper's abilities. Dommie couldn't understand why her expression was so grave and uncertain as she looked the boy over in silence. He was made even more uncomfortable when Murdock closed the door and came to stand at his wife's shoulder. The man's face fell solemn, his hands pressing against the edge of the desk as he leaned in like he was about to reveal a great secret.

"Alright, Dommie." The rapper's name had an echo on the 'o' when it left Murdock's lips. "We need ya to deal with a little problem we have when sailing these waters." He leaned in further, the light casting shadows beneath his eyes and the ridges of his weathered face. His voice grew low, "Have ye ever heard of the Blue Men of Minch?"

Aisla watched Dommie's expression carefully. The rapper shifted in his seat, swinging his arm over one side and slouching in an ease that he did not entirely feel.

"You mean that Blue Group who do those gigs in Vegas?" Dommie scoffed, his confidence slowly returning with a puff of his chest. "I don't play after Blue Men. I'm the headliner. I'll walk otherwise."

A look was exchanged between husband and wife. Aisla nodded for Murdock to continue. He seemed uncomfortable when he spoke again.

"Ya be the headliner, rest assured," Murdock replied. "The Blue Men of Minch are a different bunch. Monsters. Creatures of the deep. We need yer skills to stop 'em."

"Monsters?" Dommie laughed, leaning in and bringing his hands to his knees, "So, it's a rap battle then? My manager mentioned my old videos. These Blue Men or Monsters or whatever they call their crew can't be that good! I'll shred 'em."

"*Actual* monsters," Aisla emphasized. "Slimy Blue Men of the sea."

Dommie's laughter fell awkwardly into silence as his eyes searched first Aisla's face and then Murdock's. Their expressions were stone.

"What do you mean *monsters*? You're not serious?" Dommie said hesitantly.

"Aye, we are. Very." Murdock's tone said it all. "The Blue Men of Minch are a Scottish legend from long ago. Stories to keep sailors vigilant on the Minch's rolling waters. These tales say the creatures like to share rhymes with the crew of a ship as they pass, and if that crew fails to match the Blue Men's words, down it goes. They haven't been seen for centuries. Now ships have gone missing in those waters. None have been able to cross the Minch. Everyone disappears — cargo, crew, ship — all."

"You ain't actually asking me to believe there are monsters out there?" Dommie resisted, disbelief in his features as he began to think he misinterpreted some Scottish turn of phrase in Murdock's explanation. "Real life monsters?

Is this a joke?"

Aisla held up her phone, brightening Dommie's face with its fluorescent glow. There was a shaky video of a ship's deck, water crashing over the railings in grey globs of sea foam. There was shouting, people running about the deck. Then something impossible: blue men, with sharp teeth and slippery skin. One lunged at the screen. A slash of sharp claws, then static. Then screams.

Then nothing.

"Footage from a friend's ship," Aisla said, her expression rigid. "Afore his ship sank — with all aboard. Last we saw 'em"

"Ah, they didn' know what they were in for!' ' Murdock protested, his words so rushed, Dommie struggled to understand them. "That ship hired a poet. A poet, mind ya! That may have worked in the old days, but poets don't think on their feet anymore! But you! That's where ye thrive, lad! I've seen ye do it in those videos!"

Dommie stood from his seat, shaking his head.

"Ya got to be kidding me!" Dommie shouted. "Blue men?! You want me to believe these creatures are real?" The rapper was exacerbated by the absurdity of the situation. That video had to be a fake — a good one, but a fake. His temper bubbling over, Dommie turned dismissively from the couple and shoved open the office door, storming out of the wheelhouse and onto the upper deck with a huff. Did they think Dommie Dee was a joke? Some washed-up celebrity to send on a wild goose chase? Some fool who would do just about any job for money?

He was halfway down the metal staircase when he hesitated. The reality of his situation settled on his mind once more. What would happen now? Would the boat turn around and drop him off? He imagined with a sudden sinking what would occur if he came home empty-handed. His prospects were few and if he didn't finish this job, other opportunities would disappear once his manager got wind that he refused. Dommie Dee would be done.

Aisla found the young man a half-hour later leaning against the rusty railing of the cargo's bow. Dommie's eyes were forward on the ocean, watching the sun's reddish orb sink below the watery horizon. His expression, emblazoned in the orange and red of a dying day was bleak.

"Not packin?" Aisla inquired, leaning her body forward as her forearms rested against cold metal.

"Not leavin'," Dommie replied, staring ahead. Aisla let her gaze fall to his face and she read his expression as one who watches the waves before a storm breaks.

"You don't have to do it, lad." Aisla turned to watch the sunset. "On yer word, we go back now. The plan was daft to begin with, but the whole situation is a mess." She shook her head. "We hadn' had this problem three years ago, then those bloody trawlers come an' wrecked the seabed. They brought those nightmares to the surface. Hadn' seen a Blue Man in centuries 'til then. Not my dad, nor my grandad saw hide nor hair of the Blue Men."

"So this is a family business?" Dommie asked, trying to shift the conversation from the Blue Men charade.

"Aye," Aisla affirmed. "Been in the family for as long as I can remember. Proudest moment of my life was when I took over this ship." She let her hand run over the railing, grimy with sea spray. "But the past few years have been hard. Too costly to travel outside the Minch with cargo. We've almost lost everything; still might. Then Murdock said he had a plan. Said he never saw someone as good as you." She sighed. "I'm sorry to drag ya into this. We just didn' know what else to do."

A moment of silence settled between them before Dommie replied. "I get it," he said his tone softening in sympathy as he turned to look at Aisla. "You're on your last chance. So am I."

After this encounter, Dommie decided to play along with their monster story. If Ailsa and Murdock were paying him to battle imaginary blue men, he'd at least make a show of it. Perhaps they were superstitious, much like Dommie's grandmother had been whenever she saw a black cat or spilled salt on the table. If his presence eased the anxiety of the crew and their captain, all the better. Besides, what did Dommie have to lose in entertaining an absurd idea?

Dommie spent the next few hours indulging the Findleys' fears, trying to prepare for the impossible. He gleaned what he could from Aisla and Murdock, and learned more about their concerns surrounding the Blue Men of Minch. They never questioned the authenticity of the video, never wondered whether the Blue Men were true. They believed the legend to their bones.

Dommie listened to the old tales, told in the dim glow of the ship's small kitchen. He learned how the lines would go, shorter than he was used to, but adaptability had always been a strength of Dommie's. The young rapper was surprised at how much he enjoyed discussing his craft with Aisla and Murdock. Visions of a time before the bright lights and big deals bubbled up in his memory, when words rolled like waves across his mind, spilling from his lips as streams, weaving together in a melodic, rhythmic ocean of sound. Free from the constraints of contractual obligations and commanding quotas, Dommie began to remember a time when he rapped, not for fame, but for the joy of welding words together to create something new. He went to bed in his cramped quarters feeling better than he had in a very long while, almost wishing that he was walking into the epic rap battle his employers expected.

He was woken in the wee hours of the morning.

"Best come and see this lad." Murdock stood in the doorway, the shadows adding a weariness to his visage. Bleary-eyed, Dommie fumbled up the stairs until his footing fell on a deck bathed in the white glow of a half moon. The water was eerily still for the sea, letting a long finger of moonbeams trail upon its surface like a bridge of light. Murdock was motioning Dommie forward to where Aisla stood leaning to look over the side of the ship. Coming up beside her, Dommie scanned the waters and saw what he first perceived as porpoises. Their blue bodies were sleek and shimmered in the silvery light. On closer inspection, Dommie found their figures more like a man's than any sea creature, or perhaps something in between. Though their bodies appeared human, they had a row of dorsal fins running along their spine from the top of their heads right down their backs. They moved like a pod, their presence only marked by th small dip of their bodies beneath the ocean. They drifted slowly above the surface a moment before slipping back into the dark waters.

"Perhaps," Murdock whispered, breaking the silence, "this means they'll let us pass?"

"Naw," Aisla replied, her face grim. "Two propellers stopped working half an hour ago. We've slowed to a crawl. Now they are just guiding us deep into their domain. I think they'll stop our last one then."

Dommie was silent in the cold night air, trying to shake himself from sleep. For surely this was a dream — a nightmare even. His eyes were fixed on the sleek figures that slipped smoothly across the water's surface. He could feel his breath catch in his throat as he realized that this wasn't a dream, that these Blue Men were real, and that he was the one responsible for dealing with them. His body shook, unable to fully process the danger that lay before him in this deathly duel. His words were weapons now and he'd have to wield them wisely. Dommie chose to save them for survival. Silence was all the Blue Men would get for now. The creatures would not have to wait long.

The dawn that arrived several hours later was swathed in the dark grey of angry skies. The ocean that a short time ago lay still now erupted in chaos, crashing against the cargo ship's hull in great smacks of furious foam. The crewmen cowered below deck, with those daring enough to brave the boathouse at the helm. Aisla was there, trying to steer the ship through such treacherous seas. In this watery war zone, the Blue Men wove their way amongst the waves, threading through the water like a needle through silk.

Dommie stood at the ship's prow, now the only salvation from the Blue Men's wrath. Shaken though he had been some hours before, the rapper found that, now faced with an imminent threat to his existence, a clarity flowed through him, steadying his thoughts. It was the kind of calm felt when one must be brave unexpectedly.

Murdock, the man who had gotten Dommie into this mess, stood but a few metres behind him.

"I won't leave ya, Dommie!" he called through the crying winds, the young rapper's name anchored in Murdock's Scottish tongue "Win or lose, this fight is ours and I be with ye 'til the end of it!"

The waves splashed over the sides in great gushes, sending the ship teetering left and right. The cargo containers shook in the onslaught but remained stoic in the storm. This display was only a show to scare the crew. Slowly, the deep grey waters rose up, walling in the ship on all sides. Floating before the vessel, looking down on Dommie, was the mightiest of the Blue Men.

He was larger than the others and had three ridges of fins that ran in rows from his brow to the back of his skull. His beard was the dark green of seaweed and spread out along his chin. His shoulders were broad, his biceps overbearing. His lower body was obscured by the waves as it towered above the vessel. While he blocked the boat's path, other Blue Men peaked out from the watery walls: spectators to the sport. They lay in wait for the order to drag this ship into the depths.

Dommie did not see his audience, only the creature that faced him. He would not draw his eyes away to distractions. Fear was a futile thing at a time like this. Concentration was key.

The Blue Men Chieftain parted his salt-cracked lips and spoke:
What foolish crew disturbs our seas,
To bother me and mine.

Whether from fear or fortitude, the rapper did not hesitate in his reply:
It's Dommie Dee, come from the shore,
To match you line for line.

Black eyes blinking, the Blue Chieftain tilted his head, observing Dommie now in a different light.
You think you can keep up with me?
You puny mortal man?

Dommie's words were quick off his tongue:
You've never heard my songs before
Keep up with you, I can.

The Blue Man's face twisted up into a wide grin that showed rows of sharp teeth.

Finally. A challenge.

The next album released by Dominic Devlin, formerly known as Dommie Dee, was better than all previous albums combined. Critics praised it as an episodic adventure, a modern day Odyssey for the ears. Each song wove into the next, capturing the struggles of sudden stardom and the pitfalls that brought him to the deepest depths of his being. He spoke of his descent into darkness, and his return to the kind of rap music that had always been a part of him. The crescendo of the album was a track entitled "Battlin' Blue Men", where the hero was forced to battle another rapper in order to move forward on his journey. Several celebrity artists volunteered to read the lyrics in Dommie's duet, but in the end, he chose an artist he'd seen during an open mic night. That was Dommie's first step towards his own recording label, one infamous for helping up and coming talent navigate the murky waters of the music biz.

And every year in the fall, Dominic takes a vacation to a small stretch of land on the Scottish coast. It's a tiny community of no consequence and very few people know his name there, save two. From there, he heads out to sea on a cargo ship, spending hours on its deck, his eyes thirsting for the grey waves and saltwater air that had given him a second chance.

Shannon K Green

A gifted author with a talent for the strange, Green has been recognized in both the genre community and the contemporary literary community for his pursuits. In the past, he has been shortlisted for the 1996 Arts and Letters Award, and later won the 2015 Audience Choice Steampunk Newfoundland Showcase.

Green's short fiction has appeared in *Fantasy from the Rock, The Hamthology, Jibbernocky* and the bestselling collections *Chillers from the Rock, Dystopia from the Rock, Flights from the Rock, Pulp Science-Fiction from the Rock, Mythology from the Rock* and *From the Rock Stars*.

In 2021 Engen Books released Green's first novella, *The Snows of Aetalus*, as a part of the Slipstreamers series.

Cruising Depth

Temple sat beside the porthole in his cabin watching the water rise, then slowly darken until all that remained was his reflection. Then the exterior lights illuminated. He'd questioned their inclusion, the submarine wouldn't really need them as far as he was concerned, but one of the big thinker psychologists had insisted. "Necessary for morale," she had said, and now he was glad he'd listened to her.

"Thirty-five-hundred-meter depth reached," the captain announced over the onboard intercom. "Arrival at DSB Shackleton in twenty-four hours. All crew maintain regular schedules." He sighed wondering how he'd fill the time until he arrived at his new research station, Deep Sea Base Shackleton.

Grabbing his tablet, he decided to head to the onboard lounge; at least there he might not be alone.

He was surprised to see the day lounge almost full when he got there, and pleased to see some familiar faces. He greeted a few people he knew as he made his way to the cooler and was startled when he heard a familiar voice shout, "Welcome back, Temple!"

Soda in hand, he made his way toward Haley Lamb.

"You're looking good," she said, a smile on her face. "I guess seven months topside can bring the roses back to anybody's cheeks."

"And you're looking like you might have seen the sun recently too," he grinned. "Vacation time?"

She nodded as she sipped from her coffee cup. "Told me I had to use it or they'd claw it back. Funny switch from denying me all the time I'd asked for last year. But never mind that, how are you doing?"

"Fit as a fiddle," he replied. "Well fit as a renovated fiddle, still a couple pins in my leg but fit enough to return to work."

"Pins in your leg? Wow man, it was that bad and you came back?"

"Why would a bike accident keep me from coming back?" he asked before remembering some of the rumours that he'd had to put down in the last few days. "Wait, you didn't believe any of those stories that were going around? Please tell me it wasn't the octopus one."

"I was told it was an accident during the construction, somebody dropped a girder or something on your leg," she chuckled. "Guess I should have known better about Mr. Safety."

"Nope. I did get a few screws dropped on me when I was under last, but this was a topside bicycle accident when we were resupplying. A car nailed me while I was sightseeing in Ushuaia," he responded. "An old hand like you should know better than to trust the gossip mill. What did you get up to while I was out of the cycle?"

"A car? You sure?" she asked.

He nodded back to her. "I mean I'm pretty sure, it's not something I'm likely to ever forget."

Looking over Temple's shoulder, Haley shouted, "Giller, you dingus!" Everybody at the large man's table burst into laughter. "How does he keep getting sent back?" she muttered.

"Because he can convince people about almost anything," Temple said. "That and he's related to the owner of Triseba." At her quizzical look, he filled in, "They're the contractors who take care of the galley."

Soon people began to filter away, back to their bunks, or off to the gym or games room. Temple was just excusing himself from the table when Giller burst into the room, and panted, "We're being followed."

"Sure, Giller," Haley rolled her eyes with exasperation. "We're being followed a couple kilometers below the surface of the ocean and you just happened to spot it."

Temple chuckled. "I think you might be pushing your luck a little trying to get Haley with a new one so soon after you got her with me."

Giller ignored them as he proceeded to the nearest ship phone. "Bridge, Giller here, we are being followed," he said as calmly as he could before he paused. "Fine not followed, chased, hunted. I don't know the word for it." Pause. "Whatever, I saw a very large something off to the starboard side." Pause. "I don't know, it was big and lit up, so either another sub or the biggest lantern fish I ever saw." Pause. "Yes, I'm sure. Just take a look for yourselves." He slammed the phone back into its cradle.

"Giller, I'm not sure even you can survive pranking the bridge like that," Haley hissed the words at him.

Giller slumped into the nearest chair. "They don't believe me, said the captain will want a word with me later."

Temple looked at him for a moment. "I'm off to my bunk, try to get some rest between now and arrival. Giller, start working on your apologies now."

"You don't believe me either?" Giller's voice came out barely audible and cracking.

Haley laid her hand on Temple's forearm. "I think he might be serious this time. He actually looks terrified at any rate."

Giller looked up at her, his face brightening a little. "I know I saw something out there," he said shakily. "If one of you two would come look. Any porthole on starboard should do."

Temple shook his head and pointed to the nearest pothole. "Did it look like that?" he choked out. In the distance a shadowy figure rippled with vibrant bioluminescence.

The light pulsed faintly as the figure paced the vessel at a distance. Occasionally it drifted towards or away from the cruising submarine, but it mostly maintained a relatively constant distance.

The three of them stood dumbfounded as they watched the mysterious shape make its way through the silty water. Temple didn't realize he was backing away from the porthole until he felt a chair touch the back of his leg. With a small scream, he was brought back to his senses.

He rushed to the same ship phone that Giller had used, picked it up and pushed the button for the bridge. "Bridge, Temple speaking. We are currently being paced by a large unknown object on our port side," he said, trying to suppress the panic he felt.

"Welcome back, Mr. Temple," a familiar voice replied. "But if Giller managed to talk you into helping with one of his pranks, then maybe you weren't quite ready for—"

"Just look out the portholes, Julian," Temple barked. "At least three of us have seen it on the port side."

"Okay," Julian muttered into the mouthpiece before muffling it with his hand and shouting, "Look port and starboard and tell me what you see!"

The next sound temple heard was the handset thudding to the desk.

Perhaps ten heartbeats later, Temple heard the sound of the handset being retrieved before Julian said, "I'm going to get the captain to take a look."

"Might be wise to turn off the lights," Temple said to the multiple clicks of the handset being returned shakily to its cradle.

"What is that?" Giller said finally, his voice now without a tremble.

Haley walked briskly to the nearest portal, cupped her hands around her face and peered out. Then she shook a hand vaguely behind her. "Somebody get the light for a minute."

Temple obliged and soon both he and Giller were imitating her pose at other portholes. "How far out? At a guess," Haley asked.

"Three hundred maybe three-fifty," Giller suggested.

Temple nodded in agreement, causing his head to hit the glass of the porthole in the process. "Sounds right."

"So at a rough guess, that whatever-it-is about half again our size," Haley muttered. "About the size of DSB

Shackleton."

"About a third of the size of Shackleton according to the last update on the construction I read," Temple said.

"That's still bigger than anything we've seen living in the water," Giller said. "Way bigger than anything I've read about."

"Agreed," Haley said simply.

"The way it moves, or appears to move at least, doesn't look like a machine," Temple said, watching the light pulse and ripple again.

"I need my books," Haley said abruptly, walking from her viewing port to turn the lights back on. She found her bag and began rummaging through it for her tablet.

Temple blinked violently to adjust his eyes to the new interior brightness and looked to Giller, who was once again ashen faced. "What is it now?" Temple inquired.

"I think there's two; the one I saw on the starboard side was a different colour," he said.

"Attention," a voice announced over the PA. "All marine biology crew, report to the bridge. Repeat: all marine biology crew is to report to the bridge, both shipboard crew and DSB crew."

Haley glanced up from her tablet. "Temple, I want you to visually confirm what Giller said about there being a second one. Giller, make sure the coffee doesn't stop. I have a feeling nobody will be getting much sleep right now."

Temple made his way starboard; on this level it was mostly the crew's quarters so he went up a level to the gym facilities, the nearest public room he knew for a fact had a porthole. He always thought it was funny to call a room with two exercise bikes, a rowing machine, a stand of dumbbells, and a yoga mat a gym, but it was quicker than calling it the storage room where they kept the workout equipment. Stepping around the equipment, he made his way to the small porthole.

Cupping his hands around his face, he peered through it in the same manner he had in the galley. This time he spotted a similar shape, this one close enough that he could make out some detail. It was mostly cylindrical, with some sort of phalanges dangling from what he assumed was its rear lower half. He found himself picturing a hot dog roll filled with squid tentacles. The lights which rippled along the side were not a continuous line, as they had seemed on the other, but rather a series of individual lights spaced at semi-regular intervals. Most interestingly though, Giller was right: this one was lit in tones of orange and red while the other was lit in greens and purples. However, from the way the lights pulsed, and the bodies moved, he felt he could say with some certainty that they were creatures and not machines; no material he had worked with in his engineering career could move like bedsheets in the wind and still protect human inhabitants.

He was back in the lounge, sipping his third coffee since the creatures had been spotted, when Haley returned from the bridge. She poured herself a cup of coffee as a few other people filed in after her. "Temple, the captain wants you when we return to the bridge," she said flatly.

Temple sighed. "Wondered if they'd design to include the director of DSB Shackleton in the discussion about the discovery of a new species."

"A captain's ship runs under the captain's authority,"

Giller reminded him. "Once we dock at DSB, they're under your command, until then—"

"Yes, yes, I know," Temple spluttered. "I don't have to like it though. This whole project was mine."

Haley gave him a sympathetic look. "The plan was yours, the research facility under the Antarctic ice cap, the shuttle subs from South America, all of it was your plan. Your dream, but it was funded by the UN. It's still your dream, and you still get final say."

"But aboard any vessel, the captain holds sway and you become the head officer," Giller cut in.

With a sigh, Temple nodded. He slung his own ship bag over one shoulder and grabbed a pot of coffee with one hand before heading toward the bridge with Haley following closely behind carrying mugs. As he approached the door, he heard Julian shout, "Admiral on the bridge!" and was relieved that ranks had been established without any pointless head-butting.

"Admiral Temple, pleased to have you aboard, sir," Captain Perry greeted him. As always, their uniform was perfectly pressed, not a single hair was out of place, just as a career marine office should appear.

Temple placed the coffee pot on a nearby table and realized that was what annoyed him so much about them. Not Just Captain Perry, all of the armed forces members aboard possessed a prim discipline that just grated him. "Captain Perry, thank you for the invitation to the bridge," Temple said.

"Cut the formalities, Temple," Perry said curtly gesturing to the chairs around the navigation table. "I assume you've looked out of at least one of the portholes at this point. You've seen the things and have probably come to the conclusion that they are in fact living creatures as we did." At his nod, they continued: "All the evidence we've managed to collect indicates we are dealing with something previously unseen on this planet, or under its waters. We need to discuss possible courses of action, and soon, because it seems the two creatures are moving closer to our vessel."

"They're what?" he asked with only mild surprise as he settled in a seat. Captain Perry took the seat across from him, while Haley took the seat to his right and Julian took the remaining spot.

Perry spoke with their formal voice: "The data shows that while the movement has not been steady, they have been steadily moving towards the vessel."

"Or each other," Haley interrupted.

"Civilians." Perry rolled their eyes. "Yes, there is some disagreement among those consulted if the creatures are moving towards each other or the vessel; either way we are on a collision course with both of them."

"What's the estimated time until impact?" Temple asked.

Captain Perry turned to Haley who said, "That's up for debate. If they maintain their speed, we think about twelve hours. Based on their ability to maintain our speed for the length of time they have, we suspect that they could put on a burst of speed whenever they desire, or possibly tire and have to drop away. If only we could figure out what they're saying."

"What they're saying?" Temple spluttered and coughed a mouthful of half-swallowed coffee.

"Yes, sir," Perry said. "The pair seem to be communicating somehow."

"Not seem to be," Julian said, putting air quotes around the word 'seem'. "I've spent enough time on comms during my service to recognize chatter even if I don't know the language. The pair are making noises almost like whale song, it shows up on the SONAR as mild interference but if you press your ear to a porthole at the right time you can hear them."

"And the lights," Haley said excitedly. "The lights seem to carry some sort of message too. Whether it's a combination of the two to send the message, like vocal range and facial expression for people or…"

Temple raised his hand and the marine biologist went quiet. "So, the situation, in a nutshell is that we're being paced by two unknown creatures. They are communicating with each other, but we have no idea what they're saying. And if we keep going as we are, a collision seems likely?"

"Yes, sir," Julian said crisply.

"Have you tried evasive manoeuvres or signaling back?" Temple asked.

Perry nodded. "We have made several minor lateral deviations to our course and have been mirrored. We have not attempted communication."

Temple nodded. "Probably a good idea."

Perry nodded back. "Despite efforts from our team to argue otherwise, I thought the chance of offering offence through ignorance was too great." At this, both Haley and Julian shuffled backward a little in their respective seats.

Temple grinned at Perry. "Captain Perry," he said solemnly. "How do wish to respond?"

The captain looked at Temple. "If this was a definite hostile, I would cut the exterior lights, then dive to see what course they take. The path we follow at present is in line with the primary conditions of the mission: study the lesser-known regions of the deeps."

"But with the lives on board at possible risk?"

"With all due respect, sir," Perry said. Stopped, swallowed, then continued more firmly. "With all due respect sir, the lives of my crew and any others entrusted to me on this voyage, are more important than the orders from the brass at the UN."

All crew present on the bridge breathed a sigh as Temple responded, "Oh, thank goodness. Can we keep the sensors recording while we do that?"

Captain Perry simply nodded as they stood from the table. "Prepare to cut exterior lights and dive, on my mark," they said, retrieving the handset for the PA. Pressing a button on the console, Perry said flatly, "All hands prepare for sharp dive. Brace! Brace! Brace! Mark."

Temple felt the navigation table falling away from him while his hands, clutched tightly to the edge, confirmed that it was the world which moved. Not him and the table. The remainder of the coffee in the cups and carafes, now cold thankfully, spilled and appeared to flow up the now inclined surfaces where they had rested. The bridge, now lit solely by the lights of various instrument panels and a handful of watch lights, took on a twilit feeling as Temple's stomach retreated from his throat into its more accustomed position.

"Scanners!" Captain Perry bellowed. "What is the position of the creatures?"

"LiDAR is dark, Captain," a voice responded. "Standard dark protocols."

"Good," they replied. "SONAR?"

"No target in range, Captain," another voice replied.

"Any visuals?" the captain barked. "Camera or naked eye?"

"Aft camera shows light patterns matching the creatures," Julian spoke flatly. "The lights are flashing more swiftly, but they seem to be altering course."

"It looks like they are circling near where we dove," Haley spoke nearly on top of Julian. "Yes. They are currently circling. The lights have increased in intensity as well."

"SONAR is experiencing increased interference," the SONAR operator called.

"Is that consistent with the patterns you think represent communication, Julian?" Temple asked.

"Yes sir," was the only reply.

After a few tense moments, Haley excitedly squeaked, "They seem to be moving on."

"Heading?" Perry asked.

"Roughly the same as before," Julian replied.

"Maintain position," Perry said. "Give them some room."

"Captain," Haley said. "They don't seem to really be moving away."

Julian piped in, "Yes, Captain, I feel like I may have spoken too soon. They seem to be widening their pattern."

"Let me see," Captain Perry said as they approached

the small side screens. After a moment, a smile appeared on their face. "Put this on every screen we control. Ship wide."

Temple looked to the nearest view screen and his jaw dropped at what he saw. The creatures had drawn closer together and were no longer swimming a straight course. Instead, they were circling each other slowly, performing pirouettes and barrel rolls. "They're dancing," he said softly. "It looks like they're dancing."

Perry smiled, "Slow rise ten meters. Half speed ahead. Exterior lights are to remain off as long as we can see the creatures. Once we have a few knots between us and them, we can turn the lights back on."

They had gone less than half a knot when the dancing stopped and the creatures streaked toward the submarine. The orange hued one made contact first. A jarring impact which shuddered the vessel. The purple hued one made contact next, an almost tentative feeling tap. The orange one circled the vessel and returned with another slight tap. Then the purplish one returned with another tap, slightly firmer than its first.

"They're playing," Temple laughed as the nudges and taps continued. He turned to the captain. "How much control do you have over the exterior lights?"

"We can control the intensity," Julian said after a nod from the captain. "Basically, it's on a dimmer switch."

"Permission to engage exterior lights, Captain?" Temple asked. Before they could answer, he had the exterior illuminated. He floated the slider control between three-quarters and one-quarter in a slow pattern, attempting to mimic the bioluminescent stripes on the creatures. Soon the taps and nudges shifted down the sides of the vessel until they were dominantly against the underside of the hull.

"I think they're trying to lift us," Haley whispered in awe. "Captain, I think they're trying to tell us we're swimming too low. Should we resume the depth where we initially spotted them?"

"Take us back to cruising depth and speed," Perry ordered.

The nudges became less frequent, then stopped altogether as the vessel returned to its normal progress. As DSB Shackleton came into view on the forward cameras, the creatures swam ahead, circling the subsea laboratory, flashing frequently and with greater intensity than the crew had seen from them to this point. As the sub docked, the pair of oddly glowing creatures swam away.

"How will we report this?" Perry asked Temple as they prepared to disembark.

"I'm not sure," Temple replied. "But I know I'll have to upgrade the exterior lights on Shackleton with dimmers and hue shifters."

Bronwynn Erskine

An Ontario native currently residing in Newfoundland, Erskine is an avid steampunk enthusiast and acrylic landscape painter.

Erskine made her publishing debut in 2018's *Chillers from the Rock* with her chilling tale: "Scarlett Ribbons", returned in 2019's *Flights from the Rock* with "Feather and Bone", with "The Lindwyrm's Bride" in *Mythology from the Rock*, and was featured with three stories in *Acceptance: Stories at the Centre of Us*.

In 2022 her first novel, *By Reservation Only*, will be released from Engen Books.

Dark the Moon

The water is dark, the sky darker. No starlight penetrates the thick fog. No moonlight either, of course. The fog, and the place beyond it, only rise once a month at the dark of the moon, when all ways are open and all journeys possible.

But 'possible' is not the same as 'easy'. It's not the same as 'advisable' either, nor even 'survivable'. The ways are open. The paths are there. That doesn't mean you have to walk them.

Sensible people shut their doors tight at the dark of the moon. They latch the shutters and hang iron charms above their children's beds, and they pray if they're the praying sort. The ways are open, and it's not just human feet that walk them. After all, it wasn't human hands that made them.

The water is dark, solemn, and far too still. Far out across the bay, a light flickers. A sound, like the dull clang of a great iron bell, rings out. The light flashes bright, once, twice, then gone. The bell sounds alongside, two dull gongs, then silence. A pause, long as a held breath, then they both repeat. Two flashes. Two gongs. Darkness and silence.

Lisle, who's sailed with her grandfather since she was big enough to haul a line, knows the patterns of every lighthouse all up and down the coast. But she doesn't know this one. The mystery of an unknown lighthouse sounding through her familiar village tugs at her insistently.

If she was tucked up safe in her blankets where she's supposed to be, it's likely she'd shrug it off and go back to sleep. She has before, though she doesn't remember that. Almost everyone has. The ways sing out when they're open, calling for someone to walk them. You've probably heard them yourself, but put the call from your mind when the sun rose and the ways closed.

But this story isn't about you.

It's about Lisle, who ought to be in her little, straw-stuffed pallet rolled out on the floor beside the kitchen hearth. There's not much room in her grandfather's little house. Not nearly enough for everyone to have a bedroom to themselves, and at least it's a cozy spot where no one's likely to step on her on their way to the back door and the privy. But she isn't there tonight.

She and her grandfather hauled a drowned boy up in their nets three days ago, and she hasn't been sleeping well since then. Every time she shuts her eyes, she sees again his pale, bloated face. His awful, staring eyes, blue as the deep sea and bulging out of their sockets, haunt her dreams whenever she does manage to drift off. She wakes up gasping, sure she feels the sea pressing at her lips.

The thought of it is too much for her tonight. She's laid awake, staring up at the dark ceiling until she heard her uncle go up to bed, the drag of his bad leg and the thump of his cane sounding loud in the darkness. And then she's gotten up and slipped away, the same as she's done a hundred times before.

Whenever she's too restless of a night, she walks down to the shore and watches the waves come rolling in across the round, dark rocks of the beach. She views the sea with an old sailor's fond contempt, having been raised more by her grandfather than anyone else. It doesn't frighten her, even when she knows it should. Even now, with its moonless stillness and its lighthouse that shouldn't be there, she's not afraid. Or at least, not the way she reckons she should be. Not of the things she should be.

The sea and the night and the moonless dark don't frighten her half as much as the future she knows is coming for her. Already she can feel her body changing in all the wrong ways. Her shoulders are broader than they were a few months ago, and her voice takes experimental dips down into a deeper register. She's thought about this a lot, and before this week she's thought that maybe she'll deal with it by walking out into the water some night until she can't touch the bottom, then swimming until she runs out of strength. Maybe that's why the drowned boy haunts her so. Because that's all anyone who found her would see.

The thought tightens around her, presses her down until she feels she's drowning even with the dry, sandy shingle under her bare feet.

And then the lighthouse bell tolls. She takes a startled gasp of air, and suddenly she can breathe again. Her knees feel weak with the relief of it, her hands shaky. She thinks of sitting down right there on the beach to rest a minute. Just until her heart stops pounding against her ribs like it's going to break through.

That's the moment the ways reach for her. When she's off balance and vulnerable, and already half lost to the world, she hears a voice calling her name. Her real name. The one she picked for herself and has never shared with anyone.

"Lisle? Lisle, are you there?"

She looks around, heart clawing more fervently at the inside of her chest. "Who's there?" she hisses, choked and quiet, hardly louder than a whisper.

"Lisle!" The cry is just as quiet as her own, and soft with distance. "My darling, are you there?"

"Who are you?" she demands. "Where are you?"

The lighthouse tolls, its call muffled in the fog. The voice is twined within it in some impossible way. "Darling, Lisle, won't you come to me?"

Its light is a beacon that should warn her off from a dangerous, rocky shore, but her feet are walking her forward without a thought.

"Where are you?" she calls again, voice trembling.

"I'm here. Lisle, I'm here. Won't you come?"

A wave splashes up around her feet, startlingly cool on her skin. She gasps like she's waking from a dream, and sees she's walked down to the very edge of the dark water. The foam on the crests of the waves is bright, almost phosphorescent in the fog-wreathed darkness. She falters, falls back a step.

"Lisle, darling?" the voice calls, sweet and soft as the fog that coils loosely around her. "It's not far, my sweet girl."

No one has ever called her that. She's listened all her life to her aunt calling her cousins in from the garden in a voice like that and ached with longing to have it for herself. The longing chokes her now. Chokes off her traitorous, changing voice. Chokes off the perfectly sensible fear of the ways that open on moon dark nights and swallow the unwary whole. She knows what happens in the stories, but the longing is a tide she's powerless to resist.

"Come to me, my sweet girl," the voice croons.

Lisle's feet obey. The water swirls about her ankles, then her calves. The course fabric of her too-short trousers clings damply to her skin as the trough of a wave draws the water momentarily away from her.

She waits for the waves to deepen, to strengthen until they can pull her from her feet. She knows it's coming, knows that's the only way this can play out. But she keeps walking all the same, as the voice coaxes and croons in her ears, and the water continues to wash around her legs in playful ripples that don't grow deeper the way they should.

Once, a wave washes up around her knees and she half staggers. Her progress halts a moment as she works to keep her balance. Then the water recedes again, and she walks on.

It feels like she walks a long way, but the water still doesn't deepen. It doesn't cool the way she knows the sea should as she moves farther from the shore. If anything, in fact, it grows warmer.

The lighthouse bell continues to ring, guiding her onward, ever onward.

After what seems like hours of walking, she pauses to look back. She can see the lights of her little village far behind, on the hill above the bay. Closer, she can see the phosphorescent path she's walked across the water, with the waves lapping about it in frothy caresses. They brush against her shins like affectionate cats, though she can see the great, dark swells on either side.

"Lisle? Are you coming?" the voice asks, pleading almost.

She realises, in that moment, that she doesn't have to. She can turn around and walk back home and go on as she always has been. Except, really, why should she? What is there to go back for? Her mother hunched silently by the fire, knitting endless pairs of tiny socks for the baby she lost while her hollow eyes pass unseeing over the child she has left? Her sharp-tongued uncle and drunkard aunt? Her spoiled little cousins with their pinafores and curls, growing every day into the future Lisle is barred from? Her grandfather?

The thought stutters, stumbles, grinds to a halt. Her grandfather. The weathered and weather-beaten old man who taught her how to cast a net and throw a punch, and a thousand other things besides. The longing tears at her heart, threatening to rip her in two.

"Lisle?" the voice calls forlornly, the wind fraying it almost to the edge of her hearing. It's tremulous and half-lost now. "Lisle?"

Her knees wobble, threatening to spill her to the ground. How can she go on? How can she go back?

The sea-smoothed stones waver and soften beneath her toes, no longer quite so solid as they've felt through her long walk. She looks down. She can feel the stones, but beneath her is only water, only the deep and endless darkness waiting to swallow her down. Maybe the sea is the better choice after all. It's the choice she's always expected to take and now here it is, just a thought away.

"Lisle? It's almost dawn." The voice isn't loud. It doesn't demand, doesn't bluster or cajole. It only offers.

Water laps about her knees, a little cooler than it was a minute ago. A little more like the deep ocean's embrace.

She stares back at the hill and the village, and remembers her grandfather's patient, gnarled hands showing her the right way to tie a reef knot.

"Just like this," he says from the depth of her memory. "It's a good solid knot that'll serve you well, no matter where you go in your life."

"Where will I go?" she remembers asking him, frowning up into the midday sun and trying to read the furrows in his deeply tanned skin.

She remembers most of all how he ruffled a hand through her freshly shorn hair, the chuckle that seemed to come from the depths of his chest and enveloped her like a warm hug. "I don't know, scallop. That's not for me to see. But I know you'll make me proud, wherever it is."

With a sob catching in her throat, Lisle turns and starts to run. It's hard going, with the water up around her knees and the way slippery underfoot. Stones that aren't there shift and slip against each other. The waves tug at her legs. She runs anyway, pushing herself.

"The dawn is almost here," the distant, mournful voice whispers, soft as breath against her ear.

She can feel it. Can feel the light coming and the way

closing. Panic gives her strength, even as the water rises up her thighs. She splashes, struggles.

As the first pale rays of dawn creep above the horizon, she flings herself forward one last desperate step. The way closes with one final tolling of the great bell. Spent and gasping, Lisle collapses onto the shore. The sand is soft and warm and fine as flour as she curls her fingers into it. It sticks to her sweat-dampened skin. The sun rises, hot against her back.

Above the beach, the thick and verdant jungles of a new world wait.

Afterword

The sea is a dangerous, unknowable entity, with depths that man has yet to explore and creatures that we may never actually encounter. The Atlantic Ocean, the one that surrounds our island of Newfoundland, is a particularly vicious sea, with freezing cold waves, terrible winds, and ridiculously strong undertows. Ask any islander and they will agree that the ocean is dangerous and, depending on its mood, even murderous.

However, even knowing that, for me the Atlantic Ocean has always shown me the way back home. Whether it's as natural as the fact that my home is a mere fifteen-minute walk away from a beach or if it's as simple as seeing it every day, I cannot say. What I do know is that when travelling across this country, or even into other countries, there's a part of me that misses the ocean when I've been away from it too long.

The Pacific Ocean is different: visiting that sea is like meeting the sibling of my best friend. I can see where the similarities are, and I'm inclined to like them just on principle of who they are (unless, of course, there's bad blood between the two, but let's suppose there's not), and maybe they have the same laugh or smile, but it's still a stranger, they're still an unknown, if a friendly one. The Pacific Ocean *smells* different than the Atlantic Ocean (for those of you who do not know, take my word for it: one is cold and fresh, the other thick and briny), but in the absence of one, I will take the other.

For reasons that I will attribute to my admittedly complete bias, most of the stories in this collection I have imagined belonging to the Atlantic Ocean. There's something dangerous, something chilling in most of them, but also a freshness. And if there was a theme to be found in this anthology, it could perhaps be the idea of the strange sort of baptism that comes with finding oneself thrown into the ocean: the person the emerges at the other end of the story is not the same as the one at the beginning. There is redemption in these waves, a healing that comes from washing in the waters, or a judgement being passed by nature's own laws. When you find yourself facing the ocean, do you find danger and darkness or adventure and high spirits; and how much of what you find is only you recognizing your own reflection?

We offer our sincere thanks to all contributors to this anthology, and to every single reader. We hope, as always, that these stories inspire you in your creative endeavours, whichever form they may take. May the ocean breeze reach you, wherever you are, and rejuvenate you as it has always done for us.

God bless,
Erin Vance
Editor

ON THE COVER

The cover image to this year's anthology was was created by Graham Blair of Graham Blair Designs.

Graham Blair is an artist and designer living in St. John's, Newfoundland. His time is split between graphic design (www.grahamblairdesigns.com) and making traditional-method woodcut prints (www.grahamblairwoodcuts.com).

Much of his work incorporates folkloric themes and nods to regional traditions.

SEA STORIES FROM THE ROCK

EDITED BY ELLEN CURTIS & ERIN VANCE

The sea is a dangerous, unknowable entity, with depths that man has yet to explore and creatures that we may never encounter. The seas that surround the coasts of Newfoundland and Labrador are particularly vicious, with freezing waves, terrible winds, and strong undertows.

This collection features fifteen tales designed to highlight the strange beauty and wonderful thrill of the sea. Delve into stories from genius authors such as Lisa M Daly (*Navigating Stories*), Brad Dunne (*The Merchant's Mansion*) and Amanda Labonté (*Call of the Sea*).

Edited by Erin Vance and Ellen Curtis, the tales in this collection will leave you captivated by the waves.

Manufactured by Amazon.ca
Bolton, ON

40212633R00146